WHERE IS YOUR BROTHER?

Printed by Lightning Source, Milton Keynes, UK

Published by Crossbridge Books
PO Box 848
WORCESTER
WR6 6SE, UK

© Crossbridge Books 2011

First published 2011

ISBN 978-0-9561787-7-0

British Library cataloguing in Publication Data.
A catalogue record for this book is available
from the British Library.

All the characters described in this book are fictitious. Any
resemblance of any of them to an actual person, living or dead, is
coincidental.

WHERE IS YOUR BROTHER?

Marion Heath

CROSSBRIDGE BOOKS

Note on Orthography

As this book is published in the United Kingdom, the spelling is in most cases British English. However, because the author is Canadian, we have followed the North American pattern in some instances.

Dedication

To my amazing nieces, Anne and Margaret

1

January 1984

Ryan lifted his head from studying real estate papers at the first vibration of his phone. Counting each ring he grabbed the phone on its sixth brring.

"You're later today," he said to the foreknown voice which was uttering a string of excuses. "Okay. Tomorrow night at the usual time and place. Don't disappoint me again—I can't always be working at my office as Janet believes."

Disgruntled at the change of plans, Ryan flipped the canoe back onto its stand and wondered how his two children, Dale and Luci, and Janet, his wife, would be spending the evening. Because he worked irregular hours selling houses and keeping assignations, they would be happy to have Dad home. Maybe they rated a special treat; he would pick up pizza. Since Janet, a teacher, would be in class, he picked up his canoe and left a message to that effect on their home phone.

Compulsively, he tackled the pile of real estate transactions which were efficiently organized according to date and in their proper place waiting to be finalized. A successful salesman with his infectious grin, brown eyes and wavy black hair, clients found him attractive and honest. For his part, he preferred selling the real estate to the drudgery of paperwork.

Outside an old Mustang gunned its motor, causing Ryan to

1

peer out to see if it were stuck. When it tore off in a blue flash, beads of perspiration formed on his forehead until he wiped them in disgust. Would he ever stop the flood of memories that a blue Mustang always conjured up?

A picture of an eight-year-old flashed before him. The boy walked faster on a country road to avoid being splashed by an approaching blue Mustang. Even in the pouring rain he admired the shining spokes of its hubcaps but he jumped over a puddle and plodded on. With his umbrella angled to protect his face from the rain streaming off it, he didn't glimpse the driver. But he recognized the soft voice.

"Hey sonny, remember me? Haven't seen you for a while. Are your parents okay? I'm surprised they let you walk home in this storm. Hop in. I'm going past your farm."

He stared at Chuck, a day labourer hired last year at harvesttime. Although the worker patted his head and admired his dog, his contact with him had been brief until now. The car door opened for him to jump in.

He had been warned not to ride with strangers. Still, his father hired Chuck to work for him—surely it would be alright to be dry and out of the storm. As he hesitated the man said, "I can see your silo just over the next rise. Get in before everything is soaked."

Closing his umbrella the boy leapt in and sat on the seat's edge.

"Let me show you how fast this baby can travel." Chuck tramped on the accelerator, zooming past his home and turning down the next road.

He shrieked, "Take me home! You promised. Take me home! I don't want to go with you."

On and on Chuck drove, past herds of cows, old barns, log fences. As the road narrowed he drove into a wood lot, holding the weeping boy's hand.

The man grinned, "I didn't promise but I'll take you home after we have a little fun. Your jeans are soaked. I'll take them off for you."

2

Ryan shook his head to mentally scatter the images. When their family doctor surmised why Ryan panicked at having his clothes removed, his father heard the story and reported the incidents to the police. And Chuck was removed from his life thanks to his furious dad.

Ryan's afternoon appointment was cancelled, giving him the time to visit Gramps and to absorb the peace he found in the farmhouse in which he grew up. As he drove into its yard, his dad opened the side door to usher him into the comfortable kitchen where sunlight spilled through café curtains to highlight linoleum squares. On the rear of a heat-emanating deerhead stove, a battered aluminium tea kettle simmered. Gramps during his hours in the kitchen could reach it from his cane back rocking chair. Ryan sat down in his mother's leather covered armchair wishing she was there to admonish him to believe in himself, and to watch her bustle around her domain to give him a hearty snack. He had never doubted her love for him even though she worried about him. Two years after her death, he still missed her.

Gramps pulled his pipe from his faded overalls and sucked on it thoughtfully.

"You usually visit me the first Sunday of the month. What upset you?"

"Upset me! Why should I be upset? I'm selling houses; have two fine children; a wife."

Ryan knew his father read him like an email as he conveyed it in a simple, "I see."

Ryan stood to look out at the large barn. "I heard and saw a blue Mustang today."

"You must send those images back to the pit of hell and remember your blessings. Are you attending church with Janet? I fear you aren't—so you don't have God's strong hand working for you to push those old emotions out.

"When Wifey was alive she prayed such a strong spiritual protection around you that no attack could come near you. What a prayer warrior she was! Ever since you were abused, she

3

interceded daily for you. She knew when you needed prayer and would be on her knees calling out to God. If you prayed like that, you wouldn't become upset."

"I know. I miss her love and her prayers. Since she died, it's difficult for me to sit through a church service."

Gramps rocked furiously for a few minutes, "I miss her, too. The light went out in my life when she passed on. She longed for you to know Jesus and His healing love. Church is the place you learn about Him."

"Right. I don't need more of that garbage. It has never helped me. I stand on my own two feet. Don't preach at me."

"Sorry. I thought we were talking about your mother. Certainly you knew she loved you. I commend you for standing on your own two feet. How are your family? I have a kitten in the barn for Luci." Gramps grinned.

"The kitten can stay in the barn. Dale is enjoying the white water instruction in the high school swimming pool and is busy lifting the weights we gave him for Christmas. Are you well stocked with food during this wintry weather? The TV screen went red on the weather channel to announce a possible blizzard."

"My pantry and freezer are full. My cows are warm in the barn and the hens are laying eggs fairly regularly. I do a version of that Chicken Dance for them but they don't clap. With my memories and my old war buddies I make out quite comfortably."

Gramps moved as quickly as his arthritic knees permitted to pour hot water into the Brown Betty teapot for a cup of tea. Ryan tensed ready to replace his façade, then he relaxed.

He knew he could rely on his father's help.

4

2

As the alarm set for six a.m. went off, Janet pushed back the covers without waking her sleeping husband. After a quick comb through her mass of golden curls, she dressed and headed for the kitchen and the automatically dripping coffeepot. While eating breakfast she ran through her plans for the day for her Grade 4 class at Ridgewood School, but thought Ryan must have come home fairly late to sleep so soundly. She opted not to wake him—the kids could get their own breakfast... donned her blue coat that matched her sapphire blue eyes and left to drive to the Happy Fitness Club. The previous afternoon she had stayed until 5 o'clock to mark work and to prepare for today, thus enabling her to arrive at school just before the bell. It was her New Year's resolution to build her body and figure. At forty years, she thought she should avoid deterioration before it found her. Happily, the morning exercise invigorated her.

The price of membership in the fitness club firmed up her resolve to get value for her money by visiting it three times a week. After the first few trips, she indulged in the jacuzzi to soothe aching muscles. Since then, they co-operated through her work-outs painlessly and effortlessly. She hoped she would drop from a size 16 to a 12; maybe bleach her hair more; apply new makeup for a ravishing result. 'Come on, Ryan. I'm your wife. You have to look at me and get back to holding me in your arms. You're a great father but a lousy husband. God, I'm not complaining. He doesn't beat me or deprive me of whatever I

5

desire—he just ignores me. I'm fed up!' And her blue eyes flashed fire.

If her car had been a skateboard she would have done wheelies with it in the parking lot. Instead she pulled her gym bag from the trunk and raced into the fitness building to the locker room. Her watch indicated seven thirty. Good; she could work out for a full hour. She proceeded to don her shorts and top and advanced to open a locker. With her head half turned she swung open the door and, startled, dropped her clothes, slamming it shut. She must be mistaken; it must be a fur collar. She reopened it to see a young woman with long hair fastened to the hook hanging motionlessly.

Too shocked to scream, she waved frantically to a few women nearby.

"She's dead. Call the office." She placed her hand to her mouth in distress seeing the woman looking so young, maybe in her teens, skimpily clothed, and with bruises on her arms and on her neck. Although Janet refused to check that closely, she could not look away. She wondered how she died and why she ended her life in such a brutal way.

The police arrived promptly. Although they had sent out a missing person report on the woman, they did not prevent her death. They herded the women who had managed to dress into an office for questioning. Did Janet see anything unusual before she opened the locker? Why was she there so early? She answered in monosyllables because her distress zapped her strength.

The detective, Tony, a young man in his thirties who sported golden hair and bronzed skin, wrote down her name and address, and gave her his card on which he had written an appointment time to make her statement at the police station.

She noticed he scheduled it for four o'clock and wondered if he knew she was a teacher. He smiled, "I can always spot a teacher. Will that time be convenient for you?"

"Yes. I'll be there. May I bring Dale, my teenage son, who is fascinated by police work?" (She didn't add that she disliked going alone.)

"Of course. One of the guys will give him a tour. You've had a shock. Should I call someone for you?"

"No. I'll be alright. Maybe when you learn the details of the murder, you'll tell me how she died, and why."

"Yes. It's a way of ensuring it won't repeat itself."

She nodded and left, listening to one of the women say, "Well, as they say, he is one of the finest."

3

It was four-thirty by the time Dale and Janet drove into the police precinct parking lot. Falling snow covered the dirty tyre tracks as Janet hastened to fulfil her promise to Tony. Her stomach still churned with nausea when she remembered the young, young female hidden in the gym locker. But Dale's eyes danced in anticipation of his visit and more importantly the effect of his story on fellow classmates.

Inside the station, the hum of mainly masculine voices on telephones; the fax machines' drone; the shuffling of waiting feet rose and fell. Halfway down it, a tall young officer motioned for Dale to come with him. Dale left without a backward glance. At the detective's doorway she knocked a couple of times before Tony, engrossed in his work looked up, immediately swooped his papers into a drawer and beckoned to her.

"Come in. Come in. I'm glad you finally made it. We need your statement and I need a break. What do you take in your coffee?"

Janet perched on a chair near his conference size desk and undid her coat sighing, "I take only cream. So this is a police station."

"Disappointing, I know. The TV setups are more believable. Did Dale escort you?"

"Oh yes. A young officer commandeered him. Are those your parents in the photo with the small boy?"

"Yes," he smiled at the photo. "As the only boy with three

8

sisters in an Italian family, I received mega attention. I never had to ask for anything—it magically appeared.

"Well, my parents immigrated to Little Italy in Toronto in 1951. A year later after they had settled in, I was born."

"It was nice of you to let them settle in." Janet sipped her coffee feeling overpowered by the tape recorder sitting on the table and by the blonde giant opposite her. Studying his Roman-type nose, fine boned facial structure, mass of wavy blonde hair and his athletic body, she imagined his Roman ancestors. Surely they were centurions in Julius Caesar's conquering legions.

When he smiled charmingly as if he knew she was appraising him, her apprehension left, replaced by an unexplainable respect. But could she trust him?

"Settling in for my parents included occasional trips to relatives on their farm north of Rome. I loved the treed hills and lakes—even the outdoor privies and wells—within a close-knit community, full of family love. Despite that, the difference between my parents' cultural upbringing and mine kept me from being close to them."

"You speak Italian, then?"

"Oh yes—fluently. I love to eavesdrop on unsuspecting Italians who are cussing at the police. Very educational."

"Because you've avoided marriage, your parents must long for grandchildren."

"Oh they have them. My sisters produce infants almost yearly. Father does complain the family name has yet to be carried on but I assure him there is lots of time. First I have to find a wealthy widow to marry in order to pursue *la vie jolie.*"

Janet rolled her eyes then spotted a framed photo of a canoeist shooting rapids. "In Italy did you learn to white water canoe?"

"No, that I learned at my college here. But in Austria I canoed in wild water that was more challenging than that found in this area. It's a nerve-stretching sport."

"I know. My husband, Ryan, who's a keen advocate, is teaching Dale the basics. Dale is thrilled because he gets to shoot the rapids with his father at Edgar Gorge this spring. But with our daughter Luci he finds mixed reactions. While she's happy to be included she's more interested in the young instructor than concentrating on the skills needed."

"Will she shoot the rapids at Edgar Gorge?"

"No. At least I think not. She's only thirteen and a trifle giddy."

"Well, so be it. With maturity she'll love the waves more than the guy. Are you ready for me to tape your statement? After it's typed up you must sign it. Take your time to remember every detail, even the obvious ones you think don't matter, such as the colour of her blouse."

As Janet told of opening the locker door and her immediate panic at seeing human hair wrapped around the hook, she recalled it was a burnished brown. She thought, 'the shock gave me a photo-image that's going to be difficult to erase—along with the panic'. The more she dwelt on it; the more the girl seemed to be Luci's size and height but thinner, because the thin material clung to the body revealing curves and bones. Luci's outrageous appetite gave her flesh on her bones but no fat. 'Stop it,' she told herself. 'You'll be thinking it *was* Luci.'

With a flourish Tony stopped the tape and buzzed a secretary to type it. Patting Janet gently he said, "Try to remove it from your mind. Neither you nor I can help that girl now. But with this testimony it may help to catch the culprits."

Janet, blinking away tears, said: "She looked so young she reminded me of my daughter. She was a pretty little thing. What do you know about her?"

"We know her name. She worked the streets downtown. Probably a runaway who fell into the hands of the slave trade. She would be raped, given drugs to hook her so she couldn't run away. Probably she didn't turn enough tricks one night so her pimp who was in a bad mood because the drug seller was on his tail for money decided to teach her a lesson. But his beating drove the life force out of her abused body. What we don't know is how they deposited her in that locker—someone at the gym

10

must know, so we will find out."

After she signed the testimony they strode down the hall to prise Dale from his newfound buddies. Janet resisted an impulse to pull him by the scruff of the neck, for she found the precinct too disconcerting. Fortunately, Tony commanded: "Your mother is tired and ready to leave; let's go. By the way, I may see you at the Edgar Gorge runoff races."

A surprised Dale was speechless until they were driving home.

4

.March 1984

Signs of spring finally arrived. A vanguard of robins sang in the rain; ducks in the park splashed and mated; grass turned green overnight threatening to grow, and north of the city on the weekend, wild water enthusiasts appeared in the Edgar Gorge Campgrounds.

Loud cracking of spring ice breakup on the Grand River had been music to their ears. On the heels of the disappearing ice, vans loaded with kayaks, and C-I canoes staked out their camping spots. The sleety rain chased away fair-weather boaters unmissed by hardy kayakers who protected themselves against the cold by wearing wetsuits and other gear. Dedicated paddlers with adrenaline flowing in their veins made their run with extra care, lest they should have to swim in the freezing water.

Ryan and Dale followed the gorge road down the limestone cliffs to cross the low bridge that marked the slalom's finish line. A kayaker completed his run, pulled out his kayak and leapt into a waiting car to get warm.

"Oh boy—that water is wild. Look at those waves!" exulted Ryan. "The bigger the wave, the greater the thrill."

"Dad, those canoes are coming down those rapids fast. The current is volleying out."

"Well, it is a chute with a drop of up to four and a half metres. It's fast and it's fun." He breathed deeply, enjoying the fresh scent of pine trees, the challenging roar of rapids, and the

12

clean smell of rain-washed earth.

At the top of the hill they placed their canoes in line, with Ryan's first, so Dale could watch his manoeuvres in the water. From there the water seemed to drop into a chasm. Dale repressed a sudden fear of the rampaging runoff. Would he be able to control his kayak in the drop and steer around eddies or holes? His stomach knotted and he shivered—partly from the cold sleet in his face and partly from apprehension. Out there he would be pitted against that torrent from which it would be impossible to rescue a paddler. But he determined he would paddle the course because his father believed he could. Even as they stumbled over tree roots to the foot of steep rocks, they concentrated on frothy boil caused by the water curling back and churning like a washing machine. Ryan concluded, "The powerful high volume of water today has erased possible holes. You'll have a good run." Then father and son continued to check the placement of gates, noting a tricky one below the chute where they would have to turn immediately to go upstream through the next poles.

"Hmmm! I know who placed that one," Ryan said, looking around. "Tony must have helped string the gates. Yes, I see him. He's the blonde judge at the bottom watching to give demerit points to those who bang into them."

"Do you know him, Dad?"

"We paddled together a long time ago. Now he has entered my life again—helping out with the white water group. He's an ace paddler and a good friend."

As they walked, Dale asked, "He looks younger than you. Were you in the same high school?"

"No. He's ten years younger and he's the detective who interviewed your mother."

"That's right. He said he might see me at these races. And he's a judge. I should have been nicer."

"Yes. Our turn is coming up. Remember to ride the waves."

During the first of his two runs Dale familiarized himself with the surging current. At the top he passed straight through

13

two gates to enter the chute drop where he surfed the wave crest, letting the pull of gravity move him across and down. Other waves that sent him careening from side to side made it impossible to pass through the next gate. As the degree of drop lessened he made the uphill turn and passed through the last gate safely.

Exhilarated by the run, he felt the chilly air pounce on him when he pulled his canoe ashore. As fast as a cat at the vet's office zooms into a carrying cage, he leapt into the car to warm up. Paul, his best friend, deposited by his father to watch the afternoon runs, gave him a high five.

"That looks more thrilling than a roller coaster. From now on I'm seriously going to lift your weights to improve my stamina. I persuaded Pops to buy me a wetsuit when he gets back in town."

"Good! You'd love the run. You may need the gear for our trip to Kanabeek the end of May."

"You bet. It's a blast."

He crunched on a Dagwood sandwich while his father talked to Detective Sgt Tony, who was ensconced under a tarp that kept the sleet off and broke the wind. Dale could only see Tony's torso and legs, but he saw him touch Ryan's shoulder before sliding his hand down his arm to clasp his hand. Weird! Sometimes he didn't understand adults.

Bundled up in parka and pants, Paul helped Dale carry his canoe to launch it at the top of the run. Once the boat floated, the timer pushed Dale on his way.

Concentrating on the powerful surging water, Dale controlled his boat, turning it more sharply through gates, escaping rocks, and riding the waves like an ocean surfer. The currents constantly pushed and pulled around him and waves foamed over him as he dipped deeply in the water to force his craft upstream through the gate, then safely to the bridge.

From downstream Paul saw only Dale's upper body—the canoe covered by spray. When he glided with his paddle atop the canoe, Paul rushed to pull it onto the gravelly shore.

"Well done!"

14

"But I didn't beat Brent, the all-star athlete in all high school sports. Maybe next time," Dale promised himself.

Back in the car, Dale sagged. He hadn't been tired in the water but now he preferred to sit before climbing the hill. His father understood: "The cold sucks the energy out of your muscles. Those were good runs with lots of adrenaline to keep you going. We'll fasten the canoe and drive to the award presentation." Dale nodded his head.

Then Tony knocked on their window, "Will you give me a ride? It's colder now than in the morning."

Inside the car he said, "Congratulations, Dale. You placed third in the competition. For your first time, that's quite a feat."

"Thank you, sir. When's the next race?"

"Kanabeek in May," said Ryan. "That's the National man-made course where we'll camp out. Your mom, the girls and Paul will be tenting with us."

"Will you all sleep in one tent? I'd like to pitch mine nearby."

"Of course, Tony. And we'll have two tents—one for ladies and one for gents. Easier to put up." Ryan sniffed melodramatically, "Already I smell bacon sizzling in frying pans. Ahh, the joy of outdoor camping!"

5

Early May 1984

At thirteen years, Luci regarded herself as an entrepreneur—an elite dog walker. On her own initiative she and her friend, Georgie, had created posters to advertise her availability to walk dogs that lived in apartments in the nearby park. Grateful patrons (mostly elderly) gladly paid three dollars for a half-hour stroll. After five dogs signed up, Janet firmly stated, "You have homework. No more."

Until one suppertime Luci answered the phone and heard a weak, frail woman's voice ask, "Are you the dog walker? My name is Mrs Brown. My Toby and I live in the tall apartment building on the corner of Park Avenue and John Street. You appeared so pleasant in the photo on your poster that I thought my bull terrier would trot nicely for you. Because of ill health I often sit by my window. Sometimes I see you and your friend dancing along the sidewalk. Could you come three afternoons a week: Tuesday, Thursday and twice on Saturday? Do you work on Sunday?"

Placing her hand over the receiver, Luci whispered to Janet, "This lady is ill and can't walk her dog. Shall I say yes?"

Janet raised her eyebrows and nodded to avoid an argument.

"Tuesday, Thursday and twice on Saturday I'll walk Toby but not on Sunday. I'll start Thursday at 4:20 p.m. Are there things I should know about your dog?"

"Toby is very affectionate. If he likes you he'll be sweet and good. You'll hug him. If in the unlikely event he takes an aversion to you, you'll want to forget Toby."

"Oh dear. What kind of person does Toby like?"

"Don't worry. You're pleasant and pretty. He will look forward to his outings. See you on Thursday."

The next morning Luci entered the public library as soon as it opened to check out books on bull terriers. Her mystery dog put her into a state of alert. In one of the books she read that the breed came in two varieties—white and coloured. She knew Toby was the latter. In the photo an odd-looking dog with triangular eyes and erect ears had such a pointed face that its teeth seemed to run all around its head. Not pretty at all!

She read on: 'Today's bull terriers are playful, fun-loving, sensitive and affectionate dogs who are wonderful pets despite their tough appearance.

'Bull terriers are happiest when they are with the people they love, the closer the better. They are miserable and unhappy if shut away in a basement or kept outside away from human companionship.'

"Hmmmm." Luci was intrigued. "I won't need a muzzle for him; maybe we can play ball."

The next day being Thursday she walked down the hall to his door. Before she knocked, a dog growled—deep and threatening. The door swung slowly open. Standing with his paws solidly apart in a protective stance, Toby was restrained by a frail lady who barely weighed ninety pounds. Grey hair pinned back from her brow surrounded a sad face with shadows under her eyes and deep lines from nose to mouth as if she had lost several pounds.

"Good morning, Luci," she said gently. "I'm Mrs Brown. Toby, this is your new friend, Luci." Taking his cue from his owner, Toby sniffed Luci's hand. His mistress continued, "I'm grateful that you'll walk Toby. My health is so poor I rarely venture out—only to doctor appointments." Her eyes sparkled as Toby licked the hand of Luci who was impressed by the way he protected his owner.

"Good morning, Mrs Brown. Maybe Toby and I have

17

bonded already."

"Yes, I knew Toby would like a pretty young girl. He won't give you any trouble unless another dog is nearby. Then he'll protect you and that other canine had better watch out."

Luci had pockets full of treats—enough for every dog. Taking the leash she smiled at Toby. He was so homely he looked cute with dark grey back and upper face. Under the chin and on his stomach his pure white fur sparkled. Giving her a let's go look with his little eyes, he tugged on the leash.

"Right! We're off to Grand Park."

Toby walked, sniffed, lifted his leg, even squatted for her, earning a few pats and a treat for waiting at the kerb. 'I knew he'd be easy,' she smugly said to herself as they wheeled around a corner near the apartment building.

However, Toby did not remember the sidewalk entrance. When she turned in to enter it, he continued until the leash forced him to sit. There he sat—facing away from the building while Luci tugged, explained he was home, cajoled, pretended to walk away.

Toby sat on strike like an activist for civil rights.

No dog training manual mentioned a similar situation; she said, "We'll walk around the block once more, then go in."

Toby almost smiled but hid it from Luci. On their return he resumed his sit down stance. Finally Luci took a deep breath and heaved him into her arms. Immediately a self-satisfied, contented expression spread over his face.

A passing lady laughed, "Well, he certainly likes you when he makes you carry him in."

"Has he done this before?"

"Oh yes, dear. He rarely walks back through the outer doors."

"Ohh, he's heavy, you know."

6

The next week, Luci picked up Toby in the evening, crossing into the far end of the park just as the sun settled onto the horizon. To atone for her lateness she allowed the dog the full length of the leash to explore hither and yon and to follow squirrel trails. They led to the wooded area on the side near the other road.

Luci spotted a plethora of violets blooming in unsuspected spots that begged to be picked. With three in hand, she followed Toby deeper into the group of trees. Her mind was on the upcoming white water race and she wondered whether their teenage instructor, Jeff, would be there and if he would be happy to see her.

Suddenly Toby went on full alert. She heard different sounds —ones of anguish and the thud of blows. Not one person was near her. Where were they coming from? Then Toby prolonged a deep terrifying growl as he raced to a large clump of high bushes. Hanging on his leash with all the tenacity of a fisherman reeling in a fish, Luci was dragged with him into the foliage.

Toby splayed his front legs and barked like a machine gun. A half metre before them a pair of young men were lambasting an inert older man with pieces of iron. The victim could no longer protect himself from the blows—but Toby did. A leg raised to again kick the man felt the full impact of his teeth, sending it into frantic circles to remove him.

Luci screamed, "Don't you hurt my dog!"

One thug said, "Let's get out o' here before her screams bring the police."

"Yeah! Get this dog off o' me."

Luci commanded Toby to stop by providing him with a treat, while the thugs disappeared. Close to shock she studied the man who appeared to be unconscious. Even though he had tried to cover his face, he had a bloodied nose and purple bruises. Toby tried to lick them but Luci pulled him away saying, "Come on Toby. We've got to run for help. I hope he's still alive."

They ran toward the closest road, where Luci frantically waved her arms at passing cars. But no one stopped until a police cruiser pulled up.

"What's wrong, young lady?"

"Oh officer, a man has been badly beaten and he's unconscious in some bushes—over there in the trees. Come quickly—he may be dying."

"I'll just radio for an ambulance, then we'll go. Wait a minute."

Now that help was on the scene Luci felt her knees weakening and her eyes watering. 'Don't be a wimp,' she scolded herself as she took the officer to the man. The ambulance arrived within minutes and took the barely breathing victim to hospital. The policeman escorted the hero, Toby, home first and then Luci. However, he treated Toby with great respect—not venturing to pat him or to touch Luci in his presence.

She, however, carried him tenderly into his building.

7

May 1984

Rosy dawn spread its panorama behind a stand of trees. Noisy birds sang to hurry the daylight when Luci raised her face just enough to allow her nose and mouth to appear over the edge of her sleeping bag. Although chilly air filled their tent at Kanabeek, the sun promised a warm day. Through the tent flap she saw her parents cooking breakfast and smelled the sensually satisfying smell of sizzling eggs and bacon.

Beside her Georgie stretched and sighed, "Is it morning?"

"Yes. Put your jacket over your sweats. Let's eat breakfast before the boys down all the eggs and bacon. Maybe they haven't surfaced yet."

Laughter from Janet and Ryan greeted her remark, for the boys with full stomachs already headed to the Gull River. The girls filled their plates, munching burnt toast without complaint. Fellow campers called greetings—even a black labrador walking by on a leash barked his hello. Tony stopped by for a few minutes before attending to his official duties. The rhythm of a wild water weekend was under way.

Janet asked, "Did Tony bring a girlfriend? If Joyce comes, maybe we can introduce them." She continued wiping the table before shutting down the propane stove until the next meal. Any activity suggesting housekeeping had already sent the girls scurrying to the river.

"No, he didn't bring a girl friend." Ryan, carrying his prized paddle that touched river bottoms; that controlled his path in the

21

current and laughed at hydraulics, went in search of the teenagers.

He found them climbing rocks along the river to the top of the 800 metre white water course. A dam, built to control fast pushy water, formed a large eddy pool below it. Advanced paddlers preparing for international competitions raced from the eddy through a small drop into a channel that ran to Earl's Hole. Not keen about the frothy water, Paul and the girls tried to drag Dale away, urging him down to Earl's run where they would practise and compete with other intermediate paddlers.

"Let's go, buddy. We're not getting into that torrent this year." Paul rolled his eyes.

But Dale lingered, noting sharp rocks and hydraulic waves. What a challenge! However, he respected the river's power, for if he spilled and had to swim it would be a nasty experience. Maybe next year he could run that course.

Below the eddies of Earl's run, the river curved in a wide C to end at Whitehorse Falls. At its base a large eddy pool formed the starting point from which intermediate canoes paddled. Even here Dale realised a swim could be unpleasant. He was thankful his father made him practise his Eskimo Roll until he felt like a whirling top. Without that technique he might be forced over the dangerous Otter Slide.

Beside him, Luci and Georgie stared transfixed at the man-made course which was unlike any previous run they had seen. His dad asked, "Do you see how to steer your canoe through the gates so you're ready for your practice run? Mastering all those bends increases your river running skills. I'm a judge at two gates and I won't be easy on you."

Luci pulled a pout while Dale grinned, "You never are. You expect us to remember everything you taught us. We'll get it right."

"Yes. I know that."

"Ha! Mom says you're always more nervous than we are—we're only excited. You're traumatized."

"Whatever. Just study the water's pull of gravity." Ryan spoke to the boys' retreating backs while Luci and Georgie

22

strolled to the meadow by the woods.

Leaning against a log in the sun, they made chains from dandelions. Above them in the azure blue sky, a few puffy clouds challenged their imaginations. Did they look like sheep or like fat ducks? Luci blissfully closed her eyes to listen to the music of the tumbling water and the soughing of the pine trees. God created a wonderful world, but He must have created the Gull River's beauty just for her.

Georgie watched people coming and going along the river's edge and near the woods. Suddenly she poked Luci, "Look at that Romeo!"

Luci opened her eyes. "What Romeo?" At first she only saw the sloping meadow that ended in a wood lot.

"Over there." Georgie pointed to the far end of the woods.

Jake danced into the forest, whistled and, as in a storybook, a beautiful redhead appeared from behind an elm tree. Jake gave the wood nymph such a smile that Luci felt she had been struck in the stomach. As they walked together he wrapped one arm around the girl, kissing her hair.

Luci jumped up and marched with head down to the campsite. She ached from the top of her head to her big toes. Jake, her charming prince, prowled in the forest with a stunning beauty. What chance did she have?

At the tents she slowed down. Her mother rushed to her, "Honey are you hurt? What happened?"

Luci buried herself in her mother's welcoming arms, "I didn't know it hurt. It pains so much to love a person who doesn't know you exist."

"Come and cry it out in the car. Your emotions are out of kilter and you think you'll never survive. But you do.

"I had half a dozen crushes as a teenager, but I learned I could be fond of people without regrets when I discovered that God loved me so much. Cry it out, honey. Then coat your pain with gentleness and companionable affection. Jake sees you as a kid sister. He doesn't mean to hurt you. And someday you'll be prettier than that redhead." Janet handed Luci a Kleenex.

23

Luci's sobs lessened. "Canoeing in the Gull River gives me a high, but seeing Jake with his girl swung me into a deep low. But I'm going to still be friendly. Maybe she'll toss him over."

"And maybe we'll win the National races. Let's get a doughnut."

The boys positioned their canoes along the shore by the base of Whitehorse Falls. Dale, wearing his helmet and life jacket, domed his skirt around the seat hole to keep out water in an Eskimo Roll. When the timer shoved his C-I into the foam, with a hand on the paddle end and the other above the blade, he prodded the current like a swimming otter parting the waters.

He cruised into the eddy pool riding the wave, letting the water push him through the first set of gates. The roar before him resounded in his ears and his blood pulsed faster. Irregular shapes of rocks had been placed strategically to add to the river's dangerous dynamics. From the shore they seemed commonplace; up close the rocks loomed like battering rams. Half gliding, half stroking, he worked the plunging current dead centre.

At the third gate he powered his stroke from his diaphragm to successfully defy the current diametrically and head upstream through the gate. When he surged past one of the river's many curves, he faced directly ahead a rounded wide rock rearing high and forcing the river over it. Within a New York minute he swerved to flow through a V formed by two medium-size rocks. Even they caused sizable waves that curled and coiled as if to snare his canoe.

Both his jaw and his gut clenched and unclenched as he stroked through dancing frothy water to tackle the gravity pull of a continually creating wave. Blinking mist from his eyes, Dale thrilled to surf across the wave crest to enter the swinging gate. Unable to synchronize his entry with the outward swing, his prow touched a pole. 'Tomorrow, I won't do that,' he thought.

Now the current plunged faster, threatening to put him into free fall until his strong muscles empowered him to race through the next gate and the next. Then he dug deep to avoid upending in a group of rocks. On reaching the eddy pool at the course's

24

end, he dragged his boat out on the right side of the footbridge. Exhilarated because the current had not shoved his boat off course,, he was eager to repeat the run.

As he hoisted his C-I, Dale was surprised to see Anna, his secret heart throb, dancing along the footbridge. With her black hair in braids from which tendrils charmingly curled, he thought she'd make a lovely pin-up. She hurried to help him carry his canoe.

"That was a great run, Dale. It was exciting to watch your strong, deep strokes."

Dale's face lit up and for a moment he was speechless. At last he replied, "It's a strong current—I could have paddled better."

Anna giggled. "Hey! An Albertan went too far over on a wave, ending upside down. By the time he righted himself he had swept past a few gates. They know how to swear in Alberta."

Dale restrained himself from brushing a curling tendril from her rosy cheek. "Wow! He was fortunate to right himself—they warned us not to swim in that current.

"Would you like to carry my paddle? I allow only special people to touch it—I worked a long time for the money to buy it."

"I'll carry it like it's a winning Lotto ticket."

At this moment, Ryan appeared to help Dale. He stopped, delighted to see Anna, gave Dale a 'well done' pat and left them to their upward climb. But they weren't alone for long; out of the sun-dappled woods crashed another teenager. Brent, aware of his good looks and moneyed family, tapped Anna on the shoulder, "I'm in the water soon. Watch my run. I'll wait for you at the finish." He rushed off.

"Dale, I don't know why I told him I'd observe his run. Because of sharing council activities, we're thrown together more than I like."

"That's okay. I appreciate your encouragement. If I place in these Provincials, I'll race at the National competition." He laughed to cover a sudden embarrassment at revealing his dream.

"Go for it, Tiger." She gave a V-sign before following a path that veered to the left.

8

Ryan moved his sleeping bag into Tony's tent late Saturday evening, explaining to Janet that the long-limbed boys needed more space in order to sleep properly for their final run the next day. She listened without comment, unable to still troubling thoughts that entered her mind.

At ten o'clock Tony yawned uncontrollably and disappeared into his tent. Ryan listened to Luci's tale of woe about Jake, assuring her she would find someone for whom she would be a princess. Then he announced it had been a long day, yawned and entered Tony's tent for the night.

The breeze suddenly felt cool to the three females, who huddled closer to the campfire. The teenagers tried out their "Knock, knock" jokes until both they and the fire petered out.

"Go to bed," Janet advised. "You're paddling tomorrow, too. The air is so clear here I'm going to study the constellations. Sweet dreams."

It was a star-studded night high above the top of pine trees. Janet located Orion's belt and the big W. She interchanged the big and little dippers but eventually followed the right handle to the North Star. Vaguely she remembered tragic stories of heroes and heroines that were immortalized in the heavens.

Somewhere in the darkness young lovers strolled arm in arm, whispering to each other and laughing. A few campfires away, stalwarts sang old camp songs before being hushed. The flow of the rapids resonated in a pervasive symphony that stirred Janet's inner being.

The sky's vastness shrank her concept of herself to the size of a firefly. As she sat alone in the night she felt cold, creeping fear of loss in her heart, loneliness. Why did she feel threatened? Was it because Ryan forgot to say good night to her? A distracted coldness in Ryan shouldn't threaten her, for surely it was explainable. And she could be strong for both of them. Tomorrow's sunshine would clear away her mists of fear. With that hope she crept to the tent.

In the midnight hour when stillness surrounded the sleeping camp, Janet awoke, disturbed by a muffled sound in the evergreen trees. It sounded like "Whooo–whooo–who-who", loud at first then softer. At first she surmised it to be a steam locomotive, then she realised an owl called for his mate. The weird sound made her feel lonely. In her groggy state she curled up tight, hoping it wasn't an omen. As the owl flew farther afield, she slipped into an uneasy sleep.

When Janet awoke, Ryan and Tony had already eaten and headed to the river to take their turns at navigating the course. To her amazement, Paul and Dale were exercising with gusto. What brought on this commitment? she wondered. Perhaps Brent's bragging touched a nerve that inadvertently gave them a stronger impetus to win—Dale more than Paul. He paced Dale but he was gaining expertise, too. After their runs, she would relax, for Luci and Georgie didn't qualify to compete in these Provincial Races. Thank goodness.

Mid-morning she spotted Dale studying the advanced class paddlers' techniques to form strategies of his own. Even as a five-year-old, building with Lego, he naturally planned his next moves.

A while later, shouts from the girls by the river meant one of theirs was racing. Dale had surged past and sat by the footbridge reliving his second run. During this run the wind didn't swing the gates as much. He cruised through the first gate but had to paddle furiously to eddy out in order to move upstream.

Although he was swept backwards through a gate, he never touched a pole. Around a curve he went deep into a trough, muscling through the foam to keep on track. The rhythm in the water's power helped him. On the next wave with his boat on edge he leaned into a giant wave, carving around the gate to instantly head upstream to the red gate. Narrowly missing a hydraulic he poised on the crest and spun the canoe to head it straight down through the next two gates. Like Ibrahim on his videos, he stroked six times on the offside, then fast on the other side not only to give direction and balance but also to keep the prow above the wave crest. The water seemed faster, for suddenly he had finished the race.

Drifting in the shallows with his paddle on top of the C-I, he knew it was his best race ever.

"Hey Tiger!" He lifted his head at the sound of Anna's voice. "You did great."

"Brent finished a perfect run."

"Don't compare yourself to him. He's been canoeing longer than you have."

Dale grinned crookedly, nodding thanks. Hoisting his canoe, they walked up the hill together for the award ceremony.

After the presentations, he clutched his second place ribbon, pleased with his achievement.

When he listened, the water no longer thundered over the rocks, instead it sang. His heart sang with it, 'I go over the rocks, too.' As he congratulated Brent on winning the first place award, he thought, 'Next year I'll come in first.'

9

The rain poured down like a monsoon erasing the heavy mugginess and dumping small lakes of water in which delighted ducks splashed and cruised. Janet smiled at their contented quacks. In the early evening the rain stopped, and cats with satisfied stomachs slipped out of doors to prowl the night away while pedestrians returning from an evening walk sauntered into their homes. At the Telfer house, after Janet finished unpacking their camping gear, she swung in the swing on the verandah.

She rocked herself to sleep, waking up when a truck nearby set off a series of gun-like backfires. Her watch read ten minutes after ten p.m. Darkness had descended, making her grope to enter the house and switch on lights. Dale had decided to sleep over with Paul, so she called: "Luci. Luci Telfer, are you upstairs?" Only a secretive silence.

She hurtled upstairs two steps at a time and scanned each room. No Luci. Strange! She should have returned from her dog- walking by nine o'clock. Maybe she dropped in on Georgie. But when she phoned her, Georgie said she had not seen Luci since eight o'clock and Luci had said she was tired and going straight home. Although Janet wanted to believe Luci was dallying someplace, an uneasy feeling gripped her.

Ryan. Where was Ryan? Oh no—not two missing persons. Dialling his office she shifted the receiver as it rang and rang. Maybe he was on his way home. Oh dear God what am I to do?

She went back to the verandah and stared up and down the

street. A couple of adults strolled home and fireflies flitted in and out of her spirea bush. Somewhere in that darkness was Luci who should come around the corner nonchalantly. Janet thought: 'I'll be so happy to see her I won't even scold her.' Twenty minutes later she received a phone call from Toby's mistress.

"I thought I should tell you that a while ago from my apartment window I saw Luci being accosted by two men in a car. They seemed to be trying to pull her into it. Because I didn't want to alarm you, I didn't call sooner. I guess they're relatives, but maybe not?"

Janet felt a stab of fear near her heart. Quickly she thanked Mrs Brown, hung up and dialled 911 to report the situation. Then she tried Ryan's office number again—no answer. Without pausing she found a stout walking stick, a flashlight and a whistle to find Luci.

Luci welcomed the blackness like a security blanket that made her fold into the dark shadows and become invisible to her pursuers. The two men in their Mustang had followed her down the street after she finished her dog-walking and was hurrying home. She longed for Toby's protection when she recognized them as the two villains who beat up the man in the park. Their uncouth suggestion that she climb into the car with them made her look around for help.

At nine o'clock the street was deserted, with only spasmodic cars passing. Suddenly the front car door opened and the man lunged to grab her. He missed her by a split second, for Luci, the high school track star, had dived into a house yard and was scrambling over fences she didn't know she could climb. But the men zoomed around the block to cut off her escape, in the process squealing brakes at stop signs and revving the engine, so she knew when they had passed and she could dash across the street. Timing was the essential feat of her dashes. Because of her familiarity with the neighbourhood she knew the pathway and elusive hiding spots until she had only one more block between her and entering her backyard and safety. Panting with fear and exertion she readied herself for a sprint across the last street when she spotted their car parked with its lights off halfway up the street. They knew that sooner or later she would try to cross that street. What was she to do? After she said a little prayer for help, a quiet voice inside her said, "Wait. I'll get you home. Wait."

Meanwhile the police, armed with a description of the car from Mrs Brown, cruised the streets slowly with dim lights. The second time down the street by Luci's hideout, she gathered her courage and with pounding heart leapt onto the road. The relieved policemen drove her home. Janet, who had been deterred by the police from combing the area, hugged her as if she would never release her.

"Thank you God," she repeated over and over.

Other cruisers followed the Mustang, blocking its getaway and hauling the two men off to the jail. They would not be seen in that neighbourhood again.

The officers, having been assured that Luci was fine, stated that they would report the incident to Chief Detective Tony Moretti and left. When mother and daughter were greeted on the verandah by Tony and Ryan, Janet nodded thoughtfully.

"Are you alright, Janet?" Ryan wrapped his arms around her before checking out a dishevelled Luci for cuts and bruises. Ryan's warmth enabled Janet to focus and tune into Luci's graphic account of her flight for home.

"If you had been home, Dad, the police would have been here sooner. I was so scared."

Tony rolled his eyes and eased towards the door. "I must get back to our station to follow up the arraignment of these culprits. There'll be some stiff interrogation. It takes a while to get through their alibis to the truth. It's a relief to know you're both safe. Good night." He patted Ryan's shoulder and left.

"How many fences did you knock down?" Ryan tried to make Luci smile.

"As many as I could! Actually I don't think I damaged any of them. The flower gardens are a different matter. Fortunately, the dogs knew me and allowed me to pass through. Oh Daddy, I

31

was terrified." And she burst into tears.

They adjourned to the family room where Ryan served Janet a hot cup of tea laced with brandy, and chocolate cake with ice cream for Luci. As Janet sipped the toddy she thought, 'I don't understand why I feel so wounded—my husband is home and my daughter escaped a horrible abduction. Why am I so uneasy with Ryan? Not only will he have a valid reason for his disappearance this evening and for turning up in Tony's company, but also why he looks so dishevelled. Stop it Janet. Your imagination is running rampant.'

Still the question nagged her. 'Why did he appear with Tony when he wasn't at his office?'

"Ryan, when I phoned your office you weren't there. Where were you?"

"I must have been outside and didn't hear the phone. This cake is delicious; will you have a piece?"

Janet retreated, too exhausted to pursue the issue. All those late nights? His reticence? Maybe Mandy, her friend, was right—Ryan was seeing another woman. Yet, his shirts never had lipstick on them. Anyway, I'm thankful that he's home now.

Together they climbed the carved staircase to their bedroom—both relieved the nightmare had ended without tragedy. As she lost consciousness in renewing sleep she little realised that she was about to be severely tested.

10

Ryan returned to his house tired, tense and faced with a dilemma. The conversation with Tony earlier that morning weighed heavily on him. When he had risen from their bed, Tony had wrapped himself in his Japanese kimono watching him dress.

"This is madness. We should be able to sleep as long as we want. Furthermore, after you drive off, all light and warmth go with you. This is unbearable." He wrapped the kimono tighter around himself, speaking passionately. "Ryan I've loved you since the first time we were together. Our love is all consuming. To guard it, you must move in with me permanently."

Ryan was startled, "If it's so good why do we want to change anything?"

"Because I don't want to share you with anyone—not even your wife. You must leave Janet and move in with me. There are two extra bedrooms where the children can sleep on week-ends—you won't be entirely leaving them."

"Tony, I domesticated my sexuality when I married Janet and produced two wonderful children. Now you want to domesticate our relationship. Won't that be the kiss of death? I love you more than I've ever loved anyone, but I'm not sure where this living together would take us."

"It would cancel any disloyalty that occurs when you're torn out of my arms at 3 a.m. to return home to finish the night in your family room. You would be fully intact with your possessions and activities in one location. I need you with me. Then we can buy concert tickets together, dine out together, and enjoy a unified life. Your guilty feelings would disappear, because you would no longer feel pulled in two directions."

Tony stopped to assess his friend's reactions. Ryan looked speculative, as though he had already thought of these long-denied truths. Tony ploughed on, "Ryan, we share a rare love relationship. Go home, tell Janet the truth, and pack. Either you move in with me or you visit elsewhere."

The hand Ryan ran over his head shook slightly. Although he had long anticipated this moment, he was unprepared for it. Because he had been furtive so long, to open his lifestyle to his family frayed him at the corners. He had rationalized that he was protecting them from hurt. Now, as well as giving them pain, he would also blast away society's polite veneer of respectability.

"Don't think about it. Just do it. Otherwise you'll be like a bear with a sore paw making their lives unbearable. Your family will be less miserable this way."

As he had kissed Tony at the door, Ryan knew there was only one answer, "Yes, I'll move in with you." Although the transition would be painful, he would no longer have to lie and deceive.

Janet stretched in the king size bed, running her hand over the empty sheet by her side. Her eyes flew open. The children had slept overnight with friends. It seemed their father had also. Where was Ryan? A fiery anger rose in her. If he didn't come home, she'd explode. How dare he treat her so casually—like an unwanted stranger!

She bit her lip to hold back tears as she slipped into a housecoat and dashed to the top of their beautiful staircase. A tantalizing fresh coffee aroma that partly calmed her, restored her equilibrium. He had come home. She needn't contact the missing persons bureau. Descending into the stairwell, she remembered her laughter as Ryan carried her up these stairs on their moving day. That was in former lifetime.

With an effort she fixed a smile on her face. But in the

kitchen when she was confronted by a stony-faced Ryan, all pretence of smiling left. Even the offered cup of coffee was lukewarm. This man barely resembled the Ryan she married eighteen years ago.

That Ryan had eyes that sparkled with joy, teased and tickled her until she cried for mercy, while this Ryan loathed any body contact with her. Furthermore he appeared preoccupied, pacing to the door then back again, glancing at her with flat lifeless eyes.

Perched on the edge of her chair, she unintentionally blurted out, "Where have you been all night?"

The question made him stop directly in front of her. His determined and ruthless look left her chilled and wary.

A prickly silence full of tiny knives of suspended thoughts and feelings. Before the imminent knife-edged words pierced her, they had reached a divisive turning point. Clenching his hands behind his back, Ryan straightened his shoulders to deliver the stabbing blow.

"Last night I stayed with Tony, who gave me an ultimatum. He wants me to move in with him so we'll see more of one another. I agreed. You and I have not been close for years. You'll also live a fuller life."

Janet's scalp tingled, perspiration beaded on her forehead; shock dulled the hurt the same way animals killed by lions go into shock and feel no pain. "Why would you move in with Tony?" She couldn't grasp what she was told—her mind didn't think that way. Ryan's brutal frankness flailed her emotions, making her feel like a discarded package at the dead letter office.

"Tony is my lover—my happiness. I'm moving into Tony's apartment."

Completely devastated, she stared at him. "This can't be true. You've been my husband..." Feeling faint, she dropped her cup. Ryan quickly poured her a glass of water.

Before she could try to stop him, he headed to their bedroom where he removed his clothing and other personal articles, circling the room untouched by poignant memories; then walked down the stairs as if they were the yellow brick road in Oz. It led to his no longer secret desire—his lover.

In the kitchen Janet, still reeling, realised their innocent children's lives were affected by this drama. "You are going to tell Dale and Luci—not I. For starters, they wouldn't believe me. They'll be home at 11:30 a.m."

Ryan, amazed at this request, checked his watch. It read 10:15 a.m. "Okay. I'll tell them."

Too set on his own needs, he had never considered the youngsters' reactions. But they always went along with his decisions. "They'll be alright. I'll wait for them in the family room."

"Good. I'm going upstairs. They never asked to be brought into this world. You explain your lousy part in it." With misted eyes that threatened to overwhelm her, her frustrations boiled up: "I hate you Ryan Telfer; I hate your lying duplicity. I hate your wanting to turn every event into an opportunity for sales. I hate you for putting me and the children at the bottom of your needs; for not considering how much you hurt us. Now Buddy-boy we're going to show you we don't need you and your slippery coolness." She raced up the stairs, slammed the bedroom door and slumped across the bed, as a storm of tears broke. Pounding the bed she wept out her anger and hurt. She decided he was a rat carrying on behind her back—leading a double life separate from her and their children. Why? Why would he love another while pretending to be her husband? And a male! How could he? Rat was too good a term for his betrayal of her—he was a slug. And at that moment she wanted to squish him.

11

Ryan heard footsteps on the sidewalk, then Luci and Dale waltzed in unconcernedly. Ryan rose from his seat to face them.

When the teenagers saw their unsmiling father, their chatter ceased. Ryan motioned for them to sit on the sofa. Looking at each other to see if they had committed a felony, they perched subdued on the chesterfield.

In their presence Ryan felt a twinge almost of loss, but he immediately blanked it out. To complete the surgery that cut him out of this family circle, he spoke rapidly, "Luci and Dale I regret that my actions affect your lives. But you are young. Soon you'll be in the world making your own way. Your mother already knows I am leaving her to move in with Tony. Because we love each other, we need to live in the same home. My clothes and other articles are already at his apartment. In a few minutes I'll be there also."

Dismay and unbelief chased across the teenagers' faces. Were they hearing correctly? They felt this man with his resentful, stony face was a stranger—not their usual loving father.

"What?" Luci shouted incredulously. She leapt to her feet wanting to strike out at him. Flushed from running and anger, her huge eyes filled her face. Although she heard the words 'leaving' and 'Tony' the connection had not registered. "You can't do that! You're our dad."

"I have moved in with Tony. Your mother and I are no longer a couple in the romantic sense. Tony and I are."

37

Luci stared at him. For a moment the memories of seeing them together at the wild water races came back, forcing her to realise it was true. Quickly she erased them from her mind.

"It's monstrous. We were nice to him. Now he's taken you away from us." She bit back tears of disappointment, dreading an unknown future.

Dale, understanding the finality of his father's decision, blanched. "Does that mean you're gay? Can't you love Mom any more?" His voice rose to a squeak. His knuckles gripping a chair turned white as if his heart stopped pumping blood.

"No, I don't love your mother as a husband any more. Yes I'm gay."

"What happens to us? You say we're grown up. Well we're not. You're the man of this household. What do we tell our friends—that our Dad is a geek?"

"Tell them what you like. But I'm still your father."

"But Daddy," Luci stopped howling for a minute. "Will we ever see you?"

Ryan's face softened. "Of course, I'll see you two," he said, as if it had been obvious. "You're my son and daughter—bone of my bone, flesh of my flesh. Tony and I will work out an agreement with your mother for weekends you are to visit us. It'll be part of the separation agreement."

Dale, feeling like a drowning swimmer about to go under for the third time, stifled the screams rising in himself. Would they want to visit the pair on weekends? If they were shunted back and forth their lives would no longer appear normal.

"Dad, maybe we won't want to visit you on weekends. It's unfair. We have lives, too."

Heading to the side door, Ryan tried unsuccessfully to place his arm around Dale's shoulders. "We've worked out other problems. We'll solve this difficulty, too. Luci, I'll phone soon. You mind your mother."

In a fast-moving blur he was gone.

"Baloney!" exploded Dale. "He's not for real!" He scanned

the kitchen wild-eyed, surprised it looked the same after their lives were turned inside out. However, no tempting smells of dinner lingered in the air—only a barren sense of loneliness in a silent house.

"MOM!" they yelled, running for the stairs which they mounted two steps at a time. Maybe she drove her car into a tree or resorted to suicide? How could she not feel cut off at the knees by their father's cruelty! She had always been their stable rock; but they had thought their father was too.

They halted in the bedroom doorway. Her prone body lay very still. As they tiptoed to the bed, she turned and smiled so lovingly they fell into her waiting arms.

"How I love you! You're everything to me."

Their entwined arms formed an invisible wall that protected them from Ryan's icy abandonment. Janet's sobbing ceased. The drooping dejection of her children registering on their woebegone faces sparked a hard core of inner anger. That mean-spirited man to whom they once spoke endearments now bore no relation to the person they had envisioned him to be. But an artery to her heart that the guillotine of abandonment tried to cut through resisted the agony. Her mind kept repeating: 'he's going; he's left; he's gone' until that artery of hope was severed.

Janet took Dale's face in her hands attempting to apply salve to his wounded heart that ached for his fallen hero. "Dale, we'll suffer through this together. The pain won't last forever. Oh Dale, I don't know—I don't know what happened. How could he toss us aside like unwanted baubles? I don't know anyone who has had to rise above a similar situation."

Dale's face tightened and he kicked the bedpost. "I hate him. He deserted you and us—for Tony. Why? I can't stomach it."

"Dale, I wish I knew the reason. I don't. It's been sprung on us. I didn't heed the warning signs. This morning I had a husband. This evening I don't. Although my husband left me, he can never cease being your father. We have to wrestle with that fact."

Janet rubbed her forehead to ease a headache caused by the

certainty their comfortable lifestyle and modest dreams would not continue. They flew out the door with Ryan. Would there be another adequate life or would they live forever in the shadow cast by the men's relationship? The thought brought bile into her mouth.

Luci moaned, "I feel all torn up inside. When my cat died I thought I would pass out. But this is worse—I want to crawl under a rock and stay there. Mommy help me."

Squeezing Luci tightly she grabbed Kleenexes for flooding eyes. "It will be better in the morning. After you survive the night hours, the sun comes up even without Ryan's help. If it can get along without him so can we. And remember you have Jesus. Ask Him to hold you. He has promised to never ever leave you or forsake you. And Dale and I will support you."

Dale swatted his tears. "Mom, it won't be easy. Everything will be so different; it's almost like being an orphan. And it's a double blow because we trusted Tony. Now he's stolen our father. Who can we respect?" Dale felt completely hollow inside—devoid of all emotions. In the pit of his stomach, loneliness swirled like an eddy, leaving him confused—broken-hearted.

Luci said, "Imogene's mother left her father. Now Imogene cleans and cooks for the family. She claims it's easier than listening to the quarrelling. But you and Dad never fought."

"Oh yes, we disagreed when you weren't around to hear. In retrospect, a coldness and indifference crept into our relationship so stealthily we didn't realise it. But there are many one-parent families."

"It doesn't make it any easier," Dale said. "And I don't know of any other father who left for a male lover. What if guys think I'm homosexual, too?"

Janet shuddered, "You're not your father. You're a distinct person in your own God-given right. You've been raised heterosexual and will remain so."

"At least my weight-lifting developed strong muscles. I can defend myself against any wisecracks."

Janet furrowed her forehead. "Keep out of trouble, Dale. We'll act as if nothing has happened. Avoid unpleasant people. Gossipers will have a field day. But we'll ignore them."

At this point no words could help—they were bereft. A part of her wanted to indulge in self-pity. However, her normal, rational self believed emotional healing would come and they would find their way.

In agony she cried out, "Jesus, you were deserted. You must have felt like this. How did you bear it? Help us, Lord."

12

The ringing phone intruded on the quiet morning sounding like police sirens wailing. Having paced the floor half the night, Janet finally dropped onto her bed exhausted. When the vibrating sound persisted she stretched out an arm and picked up the receiver.

"Hello," she whispered.

"Janet, the Lord has me praying for you. I want to pray more accurately so I need to know your problem. It must be dire, for I've been on my knees since 4 a.m."

Relieved that Mandy, her best friend, talked on the other end, Janet said, "Ryan packed his clothes and walked out on me. Just like that. No warning. Just moved out."

"Oh honey. Get over here. You need ministry."

"I'm coming."

At her friend's house she stood in the kitchen where Mandy threw her arms around Janet, willing strength into her.

"We're going upstairs to my prayer room. Jennifer will bring you coffee and toast."

In the prayer room Janet slid into a battered old rocker that had weathered many broken hearts. Crouched on a stool beside the rocker, Mandy stroked Janet's hand to help her compose herself and to wipe her tears.

Rocking slightly, Janet tried to batten down her emotions so she could think rationally. Her brain felt like cotton batten. Covering her face with her hands she shook her head, determined to explain and pray. She had no other hope.

Although she sipped the coffee Jennifer brought, she refused food. Ryan's face before he left floated in front of her closed eyes. When had their marriage started to go wrong? At the time their high school friends found partners, they had paired up with each other. As sweethearts they watched a large orange harvest moon from Prospect Hill and snuggled at scarcely watched drive-in movies. Even during the year she attended Teachers' College in another city, they dated frequently. Although he never romanced her with flowers and chocolates, their days as young lovers seemed idyllic.

On an even keel they drifted into marriage. Janet assumed that as a competent homemaker like her mother, she would nurture a happy husband and family. What a delusion!

"Janet, tell me what happened. I don't need ins and outs—just why you're in this predicament. Then we'll go to God's throne room."

Janet lamented that she had been caught off guard—completely surprised. At first her emotions were snowed under from a monstrous blizzard of lies, yet gradually anger rose up at herself and at Ryan. Honesty compelled her to say they had not been intimate for two years but they still slept in the same bed. Surely they could have tried to rekindle their marital love.

The thunderbolt of Ryan's affair numbed her, dulling the pain. Still she knew it was a hidden scorpion that would surface to attack and poison her life. How would she develop strength to go on day after day? For what reason did he reject a wife for a male lover? In one morning her life changed so drastically she had to adapt and find a new *raison d'être*.

"Our lives were compatible—sharing goals, buying the house, supporting the children. If there were signs of unfaithfulness, I never saw them. I worked hard at the church, the school, the home. I did notice Ryan's frequent absences, but he always provided a palatable excuse for them. Now I realise I don't know him—his dreams, his hurts. I knew he didn't love me passionately but at times he was extremely affectionate. Perhaps that was to compensate for his passionate affair."

"Who is his friend? Do I know her?"

"His name is Tony, Anthony Moretti. A blonde Adonis in appearance. He belongs to our wild water group." She winced and her knuckles whitened on the rocker's arms.

Mandy rocked back on her heels, blowing out a big breath as if to dispel murkiness. "Woweee! You mean he has a male lover for whom he left his wife and children? Whatever came over him? The ripples from this cast stone are becoming a tidal wave."

She rose to hug Janet. "Can you tell me more about this Tony?"

"He's a detective who exerts considerable authority in his work. Apparently, it carries over into his love life, for he demands sole attention from Ryan. I've never been so humiliated."

"Perhaps you should have made more demands on Ryan. Eva Gabor regretted she had been too nice to her three ex-husbands, claiming she should have demanded more from them. That's no consolation, I know. Oh Janet, I'm so angry at the double life he led. No one suspected.

"We don't know how far he'll go if he's strapped for money. Change the locks on your house. We're going to pray for you and your children's protection and for strength for each day. God promised never to leave you or forsake you. I pray you'll be fully immersed, surrounded and protected in the mighty ocean of His love. We'll keep our eyes on Him. Standing on James 1 which promises wisdom for those who ask without wavering; let's ask. You pray—I'll agree."

Taking a deep breath, Janet placed both hands in Mandy's steadying grip.

"Dear Jesus, You know heartbreak; You know the consequences of betrayal. Who am I to complain over my husband's defection? I've always wanted to be like You. By Your grace I put my hands in Yours to walk in Your love in this mess. Pilot me, guide me, help me and Dale and Luci. Older people understand marital problems and divorce—youngsters see only disrupting surface results. Show me how to prepare them to cope with their peers. Dear Jesus, put Your arms around us. We need You desperately. Thank You for being with us. Thank You, Father God. In Jesus' name. Amen."

Dabbing at her own eyes, Mandy placed her hands on Janet's head calling softly on the Holy Spirit to flow through her body, renewing, strengthening, cleansing, healing and filling with His Spirit of love—like no other.

Savouring the healing moments, Janet leisurely sipped the coffee. Although the runaway locomotive of change bore down on her, she no longer feared the transition. Still, she wished she could postpone making needed decisions. She would survive. Her first love had moved out leaving her bereft; but only her marriage had ended—not the world. Somehow she would convince Dale and Luci that the sun would rise tomorrow morning. Would they think her cold and uncaring? Could they solve their problems? She sighed, "I hope my heavenly radar is working. I haven't a clue where I'm headed or what to do."

13

Luci awoke in the night, crying helplessly. Out of the darkness her mother appeared like a shining light, soothing her with reassurances that they would survive and eventually enjoy life once more. When Luci asked, "How will I bear it?" her mother answered, "Put your hand in the hand of Jesus. Walk it out with Him, one day at a time."

This morning, the house stood empty. Her mother must be out or she would check on her prone state. A few clunks from Dale's room suggested he was weight-lifting. There was no reason for her to get up. In her lethargy her mind revolved like a hamster's wheel. Dad said he would be there for them and they would visit him. If he really planned to care for them wouldn't he have stayed in their home? Could she and Dale trust him? Grownups were difficult to understand.

Downstairs the parlour clock chimed ten o'clock. Outside in the calm August morning, the sun already rode high. Luci heard young children who played in their sandbox wailing when sand blew into their eyes. In the park ducks quacked and dogs on their daily walk answered. In her mind the day stretched long and unending. She turned from the patio doors in time to see Dale bounce in. His eyes assessed her mood.

"Morning, sis. Done my weight-lifting. I'm about to phone Paul to see if we can hang out today."

Luci slumped in her chair. "Don't go before Mom gets back,

please. The house seems strange. I'm lonely."

"I'll make you some toast." He stuck bread in the toaster, brought corn flakes and milk to the table.

Luci sat up straight in open-mouthed amazement. Could this be her brother who always tried to elude her? He even coated her toast with butter the way she liked it.

"There Loos. Give you strength to lift weights. If you're intending to run the Gull River next spring, you start now to increase your stamina. You'll wow Jake. Ask Georgie to come over so Paul and I can teach you how to train and time each other."

Luci almost choked on her cereal. "You're letting me touch those hallowed weights! Are you coming down with something?" She studied him closely trying to decide whether he was serious or merely teasing her.

"Don't be silly. I thought you wanted to impress Jake with your wild water prowess. If you do, you must train. Paul is coming at three. We'll give you two your first lesson."

Luci's eyes brightened. "I'll become an Amazon carving through gates like Dad." She gasped. "Oh dear. Will he be doing it with us again?" Her face crumpled.

"Of course. He was there with Tony this year. He'll canoe next spring. It seems we have two fathers or something in that category." Dale sputtered to a stop. This was not easy. It was embarrassing. Without Dad he'd have to look after this scatter-brained sister. She better not drop his precious weights on the upstairs floor. He also hoped she learned the art of lifting them so he needn't supervise. Dweeb. He had things to do but she needed him—he saw that from the way she hung around him. Dad always spoiled her. His lips became a straight line. In Dad's absence he'd be a stand-in, keeping her busy, making long-range plans.

To suppress his own hurt, he determined to keep himself fully occupied. When problems arose (and for sure they would) all his strength would be geared to solving them. Perhaps by helping Luci cope, his own pain would lessen. Looking at her eating, he knew he had struck the right chord with her.

She chewed her toast dreamily. '*Wearing her orange life jacket—a good colour on her—she domed in her water resistant skirt. Her helmet snug on her burnished curls she leans forward to clasp her paddle. Only someone also in a wet suit with long heron like legs softly says, "Here is your paddle. Have a good run." She smiles at Jake as he pushes off her canoe.*'

Dale was right. She would have to weight lift. Holy horrors. What would Georgie say? Dale watched as she phoned her friend.

"Georgie, Dale is going to teach us to use his weights. You know how he goes on about needing to strengthen our diaphragms for paddling wild water. You'll do it, too, won't you?"

At the other end, she heard spluttering and: "I'm not sure, because I don't own a canoe."

"You can use my canoe. Come and time me, then you'll have an idea what we've gotten ourselves into. It doesn't look hard but we must be careful of the equipment. Dale, what time are you going to teach us?"

"Oh around three o'clock. If Mom okays my idea I'm going to apply to work at McDonald's. See ya later."

On Janet's way home from Mandy's she bought a pizza. Watching the youngsters devour it, she released a sigh of hope. If their appetites were so keen, then their emotions could heal. .

"Mom, is it okay if I apply to work at McDonald's? The King Street restaurant is hiring part-time help. It's so close I can ride my bike to it. Jim Harris who works at McDonald's says in no time he saved a thousand dollars."

"Why are you wanting to work?" Janet frowned. "My salary covers our expenses. We won't be travelling to Miami but we'll stay in our home and not starve. I don't know what your father's contribution will or will not be. That remains to be threshed out with lawyers."

"I'm almost seventeen years old. You worked at my age and you said it was good for you—you learned the value of a dollar. I don't want you to keep giving me an allowance. Maybe I'll buy my clothes, too."

"Dale, we'll talk about this. It's more important for you to keep your school grades up than for you to work at minimum wage. Can you finish your homework, enjoy your TV shows and work too? I'm not sure."

"If he works then I can, too," piped up Luci. Extra money to buy cosmetics was a great thought.

"You're underage and lack skills. If you want to work that badly start now by clearing the table. There's a couple of pieces of cake left for dessert."

A few hours later Georgie and Luci hung over her bed panting like two whipped puppies. Georgie wrapped cold wet towels around Luci's arm muscles.

"They can't hurt that much—you stalled every five minutes. That's what made your brother so mad. He's no Hercules himself."

"Well I won't complain. I hope he asks his gym teacher what weights I should use. I'm a girl and he's a boy."

"Oh yeah? I didn't know that."

Luci pushed her onto the floor, sending the towels flapping and spraying them with water.

"Never mind. I just imagine myself hurtling down the Gull River and hanging in there by my fingertips."

"You need your own equipment. Dale is pretty antsy about his. There must be bars more suitable for girls."

"Yeah. How do I buy them? I don't think Father will still indulge me? Maybe I don't need as many weights as Dale does?"

14

Janet frantically leafed through her address book. Without finding the correct number she snapped it shut and phoned Mandy.

"Hi, Mandy, you know the phone number you insisted I take yesterday because you said I would need a wise person to counsel me about worldly details. I didn't believe you until a menacing call from Ryan changed my mind. I want to phone the man if you won't say 'I told you so' and if you'll give me Pastor John's office number again. Stop it. I can hear you smiling."

Without delay Mandy gave her the number and a reminder to meditate on Isaiah 54:4-5a: *Do not be afraid; you will not suffer shame ... You will forget the shame of your youth and remember no more the reproach of your widowhood.*

For your Maker is your husband—the Lord Almighty is his name.

"Yes, Ryan upset me. He shouted that if I expected child support he demanded the children live with Tony and him half the time. I worry. Taking them on two weekends a month will be enough to uproot them. What is he thinking? With his real estate appointments he's out most of the weekend.

"Yes, I hear you. I trust your judgement. Since Pastor John counsels many people including homosexuals, he handles disputes expertly. I'm phoning him right now. Bye."

Within an hour Janet drove into the parking lot of Hickory Hills Christian Fellowship. Pastor John had given his secretary,

Rita, the afternoon off and had answered the phone himself.

"Come at four o'clock this afternoon. I've had a cancellation and it will be a treat to round out the day with Mandy's friend. She has mentioned you and I look forward to meeting you. Together we can 'put to flight ten thousand'."

His vitality surged across the wires so strongly she envisioned him like Samson swinging the jawbone of an ass to kill Philistines. She only had one Philistine to deal with; perhaps it would be easier than she expected.

As soon as she touched the door, it swung open like an electronic model except a strong arm had moved it outward, startling Janet.

Pastor John grinned at her surprise, "Welcome. Come in. At Hickory Hills we strive to make things easier for you. I'm Pastor John."

Janet smiled back, "Already my burden feels lighter."

However, she saw a furrow appear on his forehead and knew her pale face and dark circles under the eyes told him the extent of her distress. Outside the room she heard receding footsteps, a door shutting and the organ playing softly.

"We'll sit in the easy chairs in my office. If you don't mind pouring the tea, we'll drink while we chat."

Grateful for hot tea to slide down her dry throat, she perched on the chair's edge while he watched her compassionately. She clenched her hands, for sharing her story was like taking herself apart emotionally piece by piece. She had to trust him to fit the sections back together again.

"I'm here because my husband left our home to live with his male lover. Last night Ryan phoned sounding like Stalin as he made ultimatums concerning our two children."

"A breakup is distressful and painful and the responsibility of children makes it doubly difficult. Does he threaten you?" He opened his notepad.

"No. His demands are selfish and very controlling. His thinking has changed. He no longer considers the needs of the children or myself."

"In what way?"

"He demands a divorce, reminding me that half of our house will legally belong to him. On friends' advice, I've changed the locks. Apparently our marriage is beyond reconciliation. Our two children, aged 14 and 16, are less surprised, for in their world they learn that a lot of children live in one-parent homes. Divorce is so common they accept that it's not the end of the world. They ask their one-parent friends how they get on; then proceed to cope in like manner."

"Your children are well adjusted. Yet they must be hurting badly, too."

"Oh yes. Pastor, we didn't have a clue that he was gay. I was more shocked at that than at his leaving us. And I find it difficult to forgive him."

"He made the break presumably at his friend's insistence. Can you describe your reaction?"

"At first, part of me wanted to hurt him the way he hurt us. When I realised our marriage was as dead as yesterday's news, I accepted it. The part of me that had been Ryan's wife gave up and began to die."

"Was this ending as sudden as you think or had dry rot set in previously?"

"Underneath our pretences, I realise Ryan stopped loving me a few years ago. But the ache was there so long that since it left I have been feeling empty. I feel rudderless like I'm drifting in a dangerous current. His demand to sell the house means the last shred of security for the teenagers will be gone. I don't want to move into an apartment. I won't have our lives further disrupted. What can I do? He was adamant that we put the house on the real estate market."

"Get good reliable legal advice. Alexander McKinnon is a top divorce lawyer whom I recommend. Contact him immediately. We'll pray for your emotional healing and claim the fullness of God's love that heals and restores. But you won't walk in His plan for your life until you forgive Ryan and his friend. If you're willing, then God is able to birth the forgiveness in you and you will be free of all bitterness and unhealthy emotions. But you can only forgive through God's grace. Call on Him constantly, Janet."

For an instant all background noise, the organ playing, footsteps on the stairs, passing traffic, vanished. Time was suspended. There was nothing but the pastor's voice bringing understanding.

Pastor John continued, "Some of my friends are homosexuals. Like us they are in a lifelong struggle for wholeness that includes dealing with sexual problems. Lust, adultery, homosexuality are different facets of the same problem. No one can judge another person. For instance, Ryan must have suffered sexual confusion caused by previous gay experiences. The part of his self-identity that was tied to those incidents, in middle age surfaced again. He must have struggled with his self-image as well as fantasized about other men. He's not alone—straight men fight similar battles.

"The good news is that in Christ you not only don't fight your battles alone, you also fight to win. Release and healing come when you and the children keep your eyes on Jesus."

Mention of their children brought another problem into focus.

"Pastor, should Dale and Luci visit their father on weekends as he requests?"

"We'll cover them with the Blood of Jesus so no harm can come to them. Ryan has been a good father. It shouldn't be a problem."

In the quiet, prayer-steeped study, Janet and Pastor John bowed to wait for His Presence to guide and comfort. Dry, dead empty spaces inside Janet filled up with the dew of heaven. She recalled a favourite hymn:

Dear Lord and Father of mankind,
Forgive our foolish ways ...
Drop thy still dews of holiness
Till all our strivings cease

In the Presence of that healing love, she willed to forgive, knowing He would make it happen.

Pastor John lifted his head, savouring the Presence, "Soon your mourning period will be over. He is giving you beauty for ashes."

15

Under the strained circumstances, Christmas for Janet, Dale and Luci could have been a hollow celebration. Surprisingly, it turned out to be a memorable feast day, for Tony and Ryan arrived laden with gifts that Dale and Luci welcomed. Wild water equip-ment—their own paddles and wet suits for frigid spring races brought big smiles. Furthermore, the givers expected the young-sters to train using the gifts.

The men not only encouraged the teenagers to exercise faithfully, they also promised to ferry them, their friends and canoes to their swimming pool lessons each week.

In January Georgie often slept over with Luci, so Ryan could deposit them at the same place. Keen to master the skills, they huddled in their jackets, swimsuits and sprayskirts with other equipment stowed in gym bags until they heard the van arrive. While the men placed canoes on the roof racks, they roared out of the kitchen and into the car.

"Georgie and Luci, I hope you remember last year's instructions: 'Don't play bumper cars with other canoes'," Tony warned.

Georgie sniffed, "Luci's going to bump into Jake's canoe quite often." A red tide started at Luci's neck and crept upward. She glared at Georgie.

"She'll be able to trip him but not bump into his canoe. He's an assistant instructor."

"I don't need much instructing, but he is helpful."

At the pool with their slinky neoprene sprayskirts adjusted to their waists, they sat on the deck by canoes that Dad had thoughtfully placed in Jake's area.

"Hi," he grinned in recognition. "Are you girls ready? Shimmy into your cockpit and I'll skirt you in."

After Luci slid in gracefully, he pulled the hem to fit snugly over the cockpit, making the canoe airtight. Then she pushed off, barely missing Georgie but crashing into another canoe.

"Sorry," she muttered, bringing her paddle blade close to her boat to steer a course.

"Dig it in deeper. Use the power grip," Jake advised. He watched until she put her left hand on the top and her right hand closer to the blade, giving her a balance of control. "Put power from your diaphragm into your strokes."

Luci found his instructions worked so successfully she could relax and concentrate on her strokes. She even forgot to watch Jake. 'I can paddle!' she rejoiced, 'I'll be as good as Dale.'

At the pool's far end, Ryan grabbed her canoe saying, "I'm going to teach you to flip yourself out when you do a partial Eskimo Roll."

Wide eyed Luci listened. "Hug the kayak. Put your arms around it, bend at the waist as if you're kissing the deck, and roll upside down. Slap the bottom of the boat three times, and then pull on the loop that's attached to your sprayskirt and somersault out."

And she did it: rolled over, slapped the hull, tugged the yellow loop. Like an otter she somersaulted underwater and up to hit the surface. The exercise, which went as smoothly as rolling out of bed, made her feel so confident she performed it over and over. She decided that next week she'd learn to bend her body for the full Eskimo Roll.

On the way home she whispered to Georgie, "Jake is noticing me."

"He has to or he'll trip over you," Dale snorted.

"Leave me alone."

16

March 1985

During a mild spell, robins reappeared, sap in maple trees ran and the ice on the Grand River softened. When the ice broke up with a loud crack and flowed towards the distant lake, toughened canoeists returned to the Edgar Gorge to race in the runoff. Anticipating the exhilarating drop of the rapids and the swift current, they strung gates across the river for the slalom.

Canoeists arrived on the upper plateau to camp on Friday evening. Daylight was still at a premium and on Saturday they needed an early start. Tony and Ryan with his children and their friends camped overnight using mattresses and bedrolls. The teenagers, bored with swimming-pool exercises, studied the rapids' big waves that gleamed white in the gathering dusk.

On the far end of the camping site, Jake pegged his tent. In the early light of the next day, the tent opened up and from its depths like a swan from a garden pond, came a young woman with the figure of a Greek statue. Luci, continually watching the tent from the corner of her eye, felt her eyes almost leap out of their sockets. The girl was strikingly pretty in a way Luci with her honey-coloured locks could never be. Then another woman emerged to help the Venus de Milo prepare breakfast for Jake.

Luci's Sarah Bernhardt tendency enabled her to carry out her chores without charring the bacon and eggs. She even laughed over shared secrets with Georgie. She deliberately concentrated on thoughts of participating in the day's races. To her surprise a broken heart continued to pump blood.

During her trial run Ryan coached her as far as he could, then she fought alone and overcame the challenge of the waves, riding them from side to side and through the vees in the rocks. As she careened in the current, she occasionally went through a gate. Her adrenaline and the desire not to take a swim kept her digging her paddle deep while she paddled the left side then the right side. Gleefully she survived the frigid, high volume rapids, pulling into shore at the end by the bridge.

"That was fun! I had a great time out there. When do I run the rapids again?"

"This afternoon," her father replied, "You've conquered the skills. On the next run keep your mind on the gates—aim to go through them."

At the awards presentation her name was called for placing second in the girls' category. An excited Dale clapped her on the back, "Good show, Loos!"

That night, Luci curled in a foetal position on her bed and wept—silently at first, then uncontrollable sobs for her vanquished Jake-centred fantasies. When called for a bedtime snack, she refused. Since she rarely abstained from food, her mother knocked and entered her room.

Putting her arms around her, Janet stroked her hair. "That makes two of us deserted by menfolk. But take heart, you'll have a surprise visitor tomorrow afternoon. I know he'll bring you joy."

Although Luci's curiosity was piqued, no begging or cajoling moved Janet to reveal the mystery. As the tears lessened, Janet remembered her own problems. On Thursday, Alex McKinnon and she would face off with two men who not only brought misery to her family, but also were determined to sell their home. Since both men brought in good salaries, their proposal to cramp her and the children into an apartment was untenable. Her only hope was that Alex was wily enough to orchestrate a sensible settlement. Then she could sleep soundly.

The next day at lunch, the doorbell rang. Luci, attuned to dog barks, said, "I thought I heard a 'woof' when the bell went."

"Your imagination," smiled Janet. "Go answer the door, dear."

In the hallway Luci heard another "woof" and pawing at the door as if saying "hurry up and open this".

She ran the last few steps, flung open the door and an ecstatic Toby leapt up on her. She knelt and hugged him. Amazed, she saw her mother at the door nodding and talking to a strange man.

"Luci, Toby's mistress died. Because she had progressive cancer and knew she would soon pass away, she asked me if she could give Toby to you. I thought you would like to own him and said yes. Yesterday, Mrs Brown died; her son has brought Toby to you. Now Toby is yours to walk morning and night."

"My mother, who spoke highly of you, Luci, thought Toby would be happiest with you. I see her reasoning. It appears to be a love match. Although I have many arrangements to make, bringing Toby to you was a priority."

Luci felt like dancing, "Oh yes! I love Toby. I'll take good care of him. Maybe I'll teach him a few tricks."

In the family room, Toby sat on the rug watching Luci with adoring eyes. When she plopped on the couch, he leapt into her lap, cleaning her cheek with his tongue. Her broken heart immediately snapped together—whole again!

Later Luci phoned Georgie: "Toby is *my* dog now. He's much more lovable than ole Jake!"

17

It was fifteen minutes past eleven o'clock when Alexander McKinnon cleared his desk to prepare for his next client. He supposed every divorce lawyer dealt with unhappy people. Still with each case he expected mature, fair-minded contestants. He sighed hopefully as he waited for Janet to enter his office.

Janet felt she was in the wrong place. This wasn't happening to her. No one in her family ever saw a divorce lawyer. However, Pastor John insisted this man would save her money and trouble if she followed his advice.

Alex stood up to shake her hand and to motion her into the chair opposite his desk. In his expensive suit he appeared the epitome of a successful lawyer.

Dimly she heard his melodious voice say, "Although it isn't a year since you and your husband cohabited, by the time we work out the details to divide your property and to care for your children, you will be able to file the divorce papers."

With those words, the present rolled back like a wave. She studied his good-looking face in which wit and irony flared in his shrewd eyes, only to be quickly concealed.

"You make the process sound easy."

"Yes and no. The process of filling out legal papers is straightforward. Coercing your husband to change his mind about details that he dislikes may be challenging. I've recently been through a divorce with my ex-wife." A shadow of dry laughter was in his comment. "Therefore, I'll help you get your divorce as painlessly as possible. Where there are emotions, there is always pain."

That explained the lack of family photos in his office—only a picture of himself holding the hand of a handsome small boy. Janet forced herself to smile. She knew he spoke only to comfort her, but even so the words themselves helped.

"Does Ryan agree to you keeping the house? To lessen disruption in children's lives, it is usual for the parent with their custody to stay in the family home."

"He wavers on this decision. He may have to be persuaded to allow us to stay."

"Take nothing for granted, including changing the locks. He may suddenly become attached to familiar articles of furniture."

"I've already seen to that. The next step, which you say is to thresh out a parenting plan, interests me greatly. It could provide me with a convenient loophole regarding visitation rights."

"When we meet with your husband on Thursday, we'll negotiate a fair agreement."

Janet met his eyes and nodded. "I'll work on the arrangements when Ryan answers my phone calls."

Wanting to encourage her he reached out to touch her. But she was already opening the office door. She paused to say something, changed her mind and left.

On her way home, Janet drove into the church parking lot. Inside the pew in which she usually worshipped, she collapsed to her knees and contemplated the glorious blues and reds in the stained glass windows.

"I need You, God, I need You. Help me," she whispered. "Father, thank You that my children and I are coping in our present circumstances. We feel Your arms around us. In Isaiah 54 You promise to be the husband of the widow. I lay claim to that promise. Take from me anger and resentment towards Ryan, for I will to fully forgive him. I know he wanders in the wilderness. Bring him back to You.

"In the meantime may he provide sufficiently for our children

61

and not try to adversely influence them. Speak to me through Pastor John so my life still has meaning. In Jesus' name. Amen."

Her gaze fastened on the window in which Jesus tenderly carried a lamb … until she realised that lamb was herself and that He carried her through all her worries.

* * * * *

At the Thursday meeting Ryan looked smug; his lover less comfortable. Janet, pale and drawn despite their polite greetings, wondered if they were going to gently stab her in the back or whether they meant to have a pound of flesh. Inside the lawyer's office the adversaries faced each other over a polished mahogany table. This was D-Day infighting.

Ryan was late because he detoured to the police station to pick up Tony. With her replacement coolly eyeing her, she bit her lip until she tasted blood. How could she out-argue and win against both men? In unpleasant, frightening situations she had always been taught to run to the roar. In the process the fear lessened, for the surprised lion forgot to roar, according to her mentor. But she realised that these men weren't roaring—they had positioned themselves to pounce. Even if they tore her to pieces, she determined she would survive to protect her two youngsters. Hell would freeze over before she allowed them to be hurt.

She faced Tony levelly, repulsing his stare which reminded her of the stance of a tomcat ruling his neighbourhood. She knew she must be civil in order to understand this man—on weekends her children were spending time with him. His one redeeming point was his effort to bring gifts and to spend Christmas morning with them. But in war one needed to know every aspect of the opponent even when it meant probing a painful wound.

Tony, who had a penchant for strong people, admired and respected Ryan's bloodied but undaunted former wife and hoped she would not be crying and screaming accusations into their

62

faces. There were no hysterics in Janet. Amazingly, he saw an unusual strength and peace. Ryan, who was at a loss to handle Janet, had dragged him to the meeting for support. Without theatrics it promised to be a subdued gathering.

While they seated themselves, Janet poured coffee and offered doughnuts. Ignoring Ryan's stony glances that treated her like a specimen, she blocked out the men's romantic emanations as they touched fingers, promised with their eyes. If they blew silent kisses she prepared to tip the table, coffee and all, into their laps.

Alex broke the silence: "Let's resolve this business rationally."

Ryan placed his arm protectively across the back of Tony's chair. "My lawyer is working out details on the divorce, primarily finances and property. What are we discussing today?"

"Ryan, as I understand it, Janet has custody of the children. Consequently, it is usual for the parent with custody to stay with the children in the family home. Are you in the affirmative regarding Janet keeping the house?"

"No. I've thought the matter over and decided we should sell the house, thereby each receiving half of the profit."

Janet's throat tightened and she could hardly breathe. She willed herself to stay calm, not to become distraught. "That would be a blow to the youngsters. They love the old house, and each has their own room. If forced into an apartment, we would feel cramped."

"They would adjust. I have. Because the market is good right now, we might garner a top price for it."

"No. I will not agree to the sale. The children have had a double blow to recover from when you left. To sell the house means a new neighbourhood, new schools, new friends. No. We'll keep the house even if I have to buy out your portion."

Ryan leapt to his feet. "How are you going to find money to buy me out? We've sunk a lot of cash into the building already."

"It happens that I checked on the cash pumped into the mortgage and repairs. The receipts that I kept prove that most of

63

the money came from my salary."

Alex asked, "Are you prepared to go to court about this, Ryan?"

Tony whispered to his partner: "Those teenagers are good kids. If we kick them out of their house, we may push them over the edge, causing uncontrollable anger. Give them your share of the house. Do it for me."

Ryan placed a hand on his chin studying the floor for a few minutes. Finally with a grimace he said, "Okay I'll give the kids my half of the house. But if you sell it, I'll expect a share of the profit. For now, live in it."

Still holding her breath, Janet relaxed her grip on the arms of her chair.

Alex said, "Bravo. However, we are also to reach consensus on a Parenting Plan. It's twofold: when you are to have visiting rights and who makes major decisions about them."

Ryan, not wanting to commit himself in this area, scowled at Janet; but Tony's eyes widened in amazement: "Ryan, are you sure that's your wife?" he whispered. "She looks radiant."

"Of course it is," he said sotto voce. "She does look different—maybe from tranquillizers."

Tony, still puzzled, responded: "Her eyes aren't dilated."

Immediately defensive regarding the parenting plan, Ryan placed his hand on Tony's knees. "Anything that concerns me, concerns Tony. Together we'll spend quality time with the children."

"Okay. That explains that. I know you're wonderful with the kids in their wild water activities, Tony," Janet declared.

"They're neat kids."

"Soon they will be at the 'age of majority'; the ripe old age of eighteen years. As the parent with custody I have the authority to make major decisions about them."

"Having helped to rear them, I want to be consulted on decisions regarding their future."

"As long as your support payments are not in arrears, you will be consulted. That includes Tony, too." She smiled at him, silently thanking him for persuading Ryan to let them keep their home.

"We've seen the teenagers on wild water weekends and on alternate weekends. Do you agree to continue this arrangement?"

"Oh yes. They seem happy with it. As the person who has custody of them, I am to facilitate their contact with the other spouse as is consistent with the best interests of the child—according to legalese."

"I hope you don't see our different type of relationship as interfering with their best interests." Ryan narrowed his eyes, waiting, knotting his hands.

Tony's eyes, trained to detect minute detail, focused on her face. He knew that wives of homosexuals usually forbade the children to sleep over. Although Janet had not objected to the weekend visits, it was within her power to do so. The silence deepened until it hung like a fourth entity among them.

Tony watched an unusual peace flow into every line of Janet's face and body.

"I'm not worried, for I know the children are well looked after on their visits. God has promised to keep them unharmed. Ryan has always been a good father and Tony has certainly helped their wild water canoeing. I pray you have quality time with them."

Overcome with relief and goodwill, Tony jumped up. "Janet you're a special person to allow your children to visit us. You are amazing."

Janet looked upward to the One who deserved the credit.

18

May 1985

When Bruce, the manager at McDonald's, placed his broad hand on Dale's shoulder, the teenager dreaded the request he knew was coming. His head ached; his heart ached; even his feet ached. He was tired out by the influx of customers on his shift that was ending in five minutes.

"Dale, I need you to stay until eleven o'clock, because your replacement, Gary, phoned in sick. The weather is so perfect everybody is out to enjoy the balmy breezes and take a break at McDonald's. I'll owe you a favour." He patted Dale's shoulder where he had gripped too hard.

"Okay, Bruce. I'll just slip into the back to eat something. I think this is the busiest night I've ever worked."

After his brief break, Dale returned to his cash register. Although the supper crowd had dwindled, enough people queued in his line to make the time disappear. By ten o'clock, however, a group of teenagers descended on McDonald's—hungry for fries and shakes.

"Dale, how nice to see you." Since only a few people bothered to say that, he opened his eyes, fully alert to see Anna smiling up at him.

"It's nice to see you, too. Are you coming from a movie?" The glow that rose up inside him showed in his smile. He always felt as if the sun had come out when Anna spoke to him.

Tonight she wore a simple flowered cotton dress and her blue-black hair curled up gently above her neckline.

"Yes. A group of us finished a senior year council meeting by going to a John Wayne movie. Do you usually work this late?"

"Not usually. Tonight my replacement phoned in sick, so I'm helping out. What can I get you?"

"Her usual is a strawberry milkshake and fries." Brent, looming possessively over Anna, shafted Dale with a nasty look.

"No. Tonight I'm having a chocolate sundae and I'll pay for it." Anna sidled away from him.

"Tonight your sundae is compliments of the house." Dale winked at her.

As Brent carried their orders away, he bellowed loudly, "Why do you bother with that faggot? You've heard about his father."

Anna ground her teeth. "He is not his father. He's okay."

Dale's ears turned red but he controlled his temper until his shift ended. On his way out Bruce thanked him for staying on, adding, "You better watch out for that guy. He seems to have his guns aimed at you. Is that your girl?"

"I wish—but Anna isn't my girl."

"I think she's sweet on you. She could have gone to another cashier for service. Faint heart never won fair lady. Goodnight, Dale."

When he neared home, the scent of sweet honeysuckle and fragrant roses swept over him, reminding him of Anna's perfume. He wanted to know her better, but Brent's threatening presence hovered around her. To deal with the muscular quarterback he'd have to fight and Anna was the only person who would place odds on his winning.

Finding his mother in the hallway as he ran into the house, he kissed her on the cheek, "Hi Mom."

"Oh-oh, you want something. Out with it."

"Now that I have my driver's licence, may I have the Honda to drive out to Gramps on Sunday afternoon?"

67

"Of course you may. Would you like company or is this a man-to-man occasion?"

"It's a man-to-man occasion. Goodnight, Mom."

Gramps sat on the verandah waiting for him with his dog. Shep barked once, recognized Dale and lay down with his head resting on his front paws. Dale saw green fields of winter wheat at the back and looked at the lawn and driveway in the front. Near the fading red barn with its cement ramp a flock of hens pecked the ground for bugs.

"Glad to see you," Gramps called. "Come and sit. Then I'll show you the new calves. How are you, son?"

Sucking on his pipe he watched this boy whom he helped nurture. Dale saw him checking his height and leanness—every inch he grew seemed to take pounds off his body.

"You're becoming a young man, driving a car and working."

"I started to drive on your tractors. A car is just faster. How are you, Gramps?"

"Well my arthritis is doing well but I can't complain. You have a troubled look."

Dale loved Gramps with his bald head, square jaw and penetrating eyes almost hidden under bushy eyebrows. A true man of the soil, he gauged the weather by his arthritis and by holding a wet finger in the wind. If anyone could advise him, Gramps could. Even as a child he believed Gramps knew the answers.

Dale swallowed. "I might be in love."

"Good. Does she like you?"

"Kind of. At least she seems happy to see me when we bump into each other."

"What do you mean—'kind of'? She either does or she doesn't. Your grandmother, bless her soul, let me know for sure. But then it was wartime. I was so handsome in my uniform." He waited for Dale's grin before continuing. "When I was on leave, she met me at the train station and gave me the warmest welcome. Tell me about this gel. I see she has crept under your

68

skin."

"Anna is intelligent, popular and beautiful. She works on the School Council—which makes problems because one member also likes her. Brent, the star quarterback, has most of the girls drooling over him."

"But Anna doesn't. I like her already."

"When she's in McDonald's she always comes to my cash register but I haven't asked her for a date, yet."

Gramps looked grim. "How are your peers reacting to your family crisis?"

"Paul knows I'm straight and tells others to shove it if they harass me. Brent, in his exalted position, is the one who belittles me. He hurts me by calling Dad a faggot and other rotten names. My anger is building. One day I'll give him a knuckle sandwich." He stood up, hands in jean pockets and kicked a stone.

"And he loves to call you the same names, doesn't he?"

Gramps put down his uncooperative pipe to lean forward wordlessly shaking his head. He knew gossips would assume that his son's son had the same sexual orientation. Watching him, Dale knew he missed Wifey, as he called Dale's grandmother. They had always talked everything over before deciding on a course of action.

"Have you enough meat on your bones to challenge the muscular quarterback? He's trying to provoke you into hitting him so he can show Anna his superiority. Do you want that?"

"I may be lean but I'm wiry. I'm equal to the contest of heavy rapids since I weight-lift most days. If I'm mad enough I can bloody his elegant nose. Anna hasn't anything to do with this even though he thinks she's his girl."

"I'm proud you stick up for your dad. You know who he is as your father even if he's screwed up. It's difficult but I'm confident that your inner strength will grow until you look Brent in the eye without shame. It's called the Jesus way as opposed to the medieval way of calling people out for a duel to protect someone's honour. Let's check the calves."

"It would be satisfying to flatten him on the floor."

Gramps shook his head. "A black eye and bloody nose isn't good. Play it cool. But if you are intent on rearranging his face, let me give you a few lessons in fighting. I fought as a commando in the war."

"Great. After the barn tour, give me a lesson. If one of us is going to have their face rearranged, I prefer it to be Brent."

"You're on. What if I knock you out? Look at the width and muscle strength in my hands. I'll fill a pail with sand for you to take home. You keep punching your fist into it to build power."

Gramps marched as erect as in his soldiering days. On a cleared section of the barn floor he gave Dale his first lesson. They worked on his ability to bounce on the balls of his feet for lightness and swiftness, then gradually worked in intricate steps.

"You have to be a dancer to be a fighter."

"I realise that. I should have taken Highland dancing when Mom pushed it."

"You'll be fine. Come back once or, if possible, twice a week all summer. Remember never to punch someone in anger. And I want to meet Anna."

"I'll be here for lessons. Anna? Who knows?"

19

The sun shone full on Dale's face as he drowsed peacefully until a downstairs door slammed. With a start he opened his eyes to see his alarm clock registering eight o'clock. Since today Dad came to take him and Luci for the weekend, he stumbled to the bathroom wishing it was Monday—not a Saturday with the lover boys.

He dreaded the weekend spent nose-to-nose in their father's apartment. If they were canoeing it would be fun rather than being there with nothing to do. They had to make it a satisfactory weekend so Mom wouldn't worry. If he could hate Tony it would be easier. But he was okay until he made eyes at Dad; then it grew embarrassing.

He stuffed jeans, underwear, pyjamas, essentials into his sports bag. Dad's van hadn't arrived yet, giving him time to tear downstairs with the bag and to eat a quick breakfast. While he munched on toast and strawberry jam, Luci yelled, "Dale, they're here! Can you help me carry Toby's food and dishes to the van? If you do, he'll be nice to you."

"Okay, okay. I hope you're not taking a ton of food."

Luci ignored him while like a queen she led Toby on his leash and dragged her suitcase. Dale managed to lug two other bags as they yelled "goodbye" to their silent mother who watched from the hallway.

"Have a good time, you two."

Ryan, looking fit in a red cap and new sports jacket, hugged

Luci, patted Dale and opened the door for Toby, who was on his best behaviour. Car rides rated high on his list of social activities. Luci gave him the space by the back window where his little triangular eyes spotted every squirrel.

Tony smiled. "I hope you brought enough food so he won't nibble on us."

"Don't worry; he's very affectionate."

"Wait till you see *how* affectionate." Dale was watching street signs to remember the route to Dad's new apartment. Finally the van rounded a corner, then pulled up to a fourplex.

Tony looked at Ryan. "Are dogs allowed?"

"They are now. It would be better, though, if you train Toby not to bark when people come and go in the central hallway."

"Okay, Dad. He'll be good—most of the time," said Luci.

"When won't he be good?"

"When Dale teases him."

In the fourplex, the teenagers settled into their own bedrooms —smaller than at home but private. At once, Luci decided to take Toby for a walk; but the adults disapproved. She lifted her determined nose in the air, "I give Toby regular exercise."

"Luci," Tony explained, "we don't want you to get lost or meet any dogs that might attack Toby. I'll walk with you. Like Toby, I need exercise."

Although Luci intended to jog in hopes Tony would be too winded to chatter, Toby delighted in pausing to sniff scents of other hounds. When two blocks over they encountered the actual animal—a German shepherd whose owner struggled to keep him on a short leash away from the terrier. Toby, who rarely sought a standoff but never ran from one, emitted menacing guttural growls. Fortunately, Tony commandeered the dog's leash with a strong arm and walked Toby until his fur lay down.

"Toby knows all our neighbourhood dogs. It's the surprises he dislikes," Luci explained.

"When my sister was your age, she reacted as you do."

"How d'you mean?"

"One minute a girl, the next a young lady."

72

Tony scored a hit with that remark. The rest of the walk she filled his ears with news about her teachers.

Ryan marvelled at his son's maturity. In height he had shot up until he stood only five centimetres shorter than his father. In a few months he would be taller than his father. Did he understand Ryan's decision to leave his mother? If Ryan explained his actions were something he couldn't control, would his son lose the last shred of respect for him?

"Dad, I visited Gramps last Sunday. He misses you but claims he knows you well enough to not judge."

"My father is something I'll never be: a wonderful man of faith. I phone him regularly to lessen his worry. Do you understand this situation?"

Dale studied a spot on the floor. "No, I don't understand. I thought we were a normal family. Now we aren't even a family. How can you expect us to understand? We tell friends you live together—not that you're lovers. They wouldn't understand either."

Ryan slumped, unable to meet Dale's angry eyes, and strove to find the right answer. Although he knew he owed Dale an explanation, he worried that if he explained his actions, his son might reject him. He determined to remain friends with Dale until he found his own life's path. Finally the silence stretched overpoweringly. He took a deep breath; regardless of the results he would speak honestly.

"After the shame of being raped by the transient passed, I discovered an attraction for men. At first I didn't know what it was but it felt comfortable. In my fantasies I kissed attractive men—never women. Girls seemed unapproachable."

"Then why did you marry Mom and have children?"

"Because your mother belonged to my youth group. The activities threw us together often. She found me handsome, fun, easy-going; hence, we paired up. It was a long time before I kissed her. Even then I wasn't as passionate as she probably wished…

"We had a workable marriage; youth and nature kept it going in the beginning. As long as we shared mutual interests such as you and Luci, and kindnesses, we had good companionship. Then more and more I felt a hollow emptiness, causing me to seek homosexual friends. This time around I responded to Tony's acceptance of me as I am.. I've needed to be who and what I am. Please try to understand; my love for Tony doesn't make my love for you any less."

He knelt beside his son, who sat with his head down. He shivered as if from a chill; but Ryan sensed Dale didn't want to hurt him.

At last, Dale raised his head. Kneeling beside his dad, he hugged him.

With the afternoon looming ahead of them, Ryan looked at movies listed in the newspaper, marking a few that he knew Janet would not object to, before passing the paper to Dale to choose. By the time the other two returned they had decided to push the Dean Martin and Jerry Lewis movie as a possibility.

"Right," Tony agreed. "I'll pop a few hotdogs in the microwave and we'll catch the one-thirty matinée. Does Toby eat hot dogs too?"

"No!" Dad and Dale chorused.

After lunch, Ryan hugged and kissed Tony even though Luci looked dismayed and Dale ducked behind the paper.

Ryan turned to them. "If you need anything be sure and tell us."

When they arrived at the movie theatre, Luci sat beside Tony and Dale next to Ryan. With kids everywhere, under the seats and over the seats, the men held hands, laughing even during the non-funny parts.

By the next morning, the constant show of affection between Dad and Tony was infuriating the youngsters. No one spoke of attending church. Instead they ate a leisurely gourmet brunch cooked by Tony.

At the tenth time of Ryan repeating his refrain: "What do you

74

need?" Dale exploded: "Just don't kiss in front of us! We're in high school now! I have fuzz on my cheeks. And we've made up our minds: I like girls and Luci likes boys. We don't want to be different. The only people we want to see kissing are boys and girls! Not boys kissing boys. We want to see boys kissing girls! Do you get it? We're teenagers."

An upset Luci stood beside him. "Why don't you two act your age? You can kiss all you want when we're not here!" They stamped out, Toby following.

A flabbergasted Ryan's knees buckled as he looked at Tony to assess his reaction. He didn't want his sweetheart hurt; neither did he want to lose his children—too much of his life was invested in them. But his primary love was Tony. If he took offence he would reprimand his children. He breathed again when Tony smiled, shaking his head, "Spunk in that one. At his age I'd have felt the same. From now on we demonstrate our affection when they aren't around. Agreed?"

Ryan nodded.

20

Two Weeks Later

Saturday morning Janet woke early. She hastily pulled on jeans and a T-shirt, bounded down the back stairs and out the patio doors to inhale freshly scented morning air and to applaud the chorus of singing birds as she walked barefoot on dewy grass.

The city had been built in a fruit-growing area: old pear trees in her backyard were laden with pears on which house finches, warblers and robins dined. Janet, watching them from a lounge chair, coffee cup in hand, silently commanded them not to squirt on her car. Then, having finished her coffee, she decided she'd been dumped on so much recently that she didn't care. Besides, God was there for her.

She further reflected that when she kept His Word, her mind stayed on Him—the Person who took care of the store. She thanked Jesus for protecting her children with His blood, especially on their weekend visits. Job's statement that what he had feared had come upon him had warned her not to worry, so she even thanked God for Job and his warning.

Although Dale and Luci visited their father today, Luci slept at Georgie's last night. On weekends her loyalty had been stretched between love for her father and her need to be with Georgie, whose support of Luci at school had made them like sisters. Whoever should pick them up had to drive to Georgie's.

Janet hoped Ryan didn't come for Dale; his swordlike stare pierced straight through her. He was so uncomfortable in her presence she wondered about his inner state. Would they ever be able to communicate as normal persons? Perhaps if she reacted as a deserted wife usually did, he'd know how to relate to her.

She was objective and pleasant with Tony even though she thought he overrated his good looks. How could he be so demanding that he made Ryan leave his family? Maybe it was 70% Ryan and 30% Tony. Well, if Ryan had to leave them for a male lover, he chose someone with impeccable manners. But she never knew what to say to Tony. He was a conundrum—he lived a different lifestyle from hers but expressed admiration for her. Was he for real?

Dale sniffed the aroma of sizzling bacon and eggs, pulled the toast out of the toaster, then sat down to eat. "Mom, Dad and Tony are taking us to a league baseball game this aft. Our team won most of the games this season so I expect they'll win this one. Dweeb! There's the doorbell. He's early."

"I'll just tell him I'll be ready in a New York minute."

Tony followed Janet into the kitchen saying, "Good morning lovely lady. I already have the news we pick Luci up at Georgie's." He grinned. "Are there any instructions for the two imps this weekend?"

He longed to ask Janet why she'd forgiven Ryan and himself, even before he'd tried to make amends, and why she greeted him smiling and radiant. She obviously regarded him as a responsible adult—not as the man who stole her husband. It should make no difference what she thought of him, but it did.

She neither complained nor accused. She was magnificent. In the expression of her eyes and lips he saw inner beauty. Every visit he noted her radiance increased like a light fixture to which more bulbs were attached. What was her secret? He knew her multiple problems. What he didn't grasp was her source of strength. How could she be so calm and peaceful?

77

"Tony, I expect them to behave. They're not trouble makers. If they're bothered by something, Dale will tell you—Luci holds back. But I think you're considerate of them and their needs. That's good."

"They're fun kids. Fortunately, I already knew them from the white water weekends. Even Toby accepts me—hasn't bitten me yet."

"That sop. He's all over everyone. But if a stranger crosses his eyes at Luci, he protects her until they back away. He's a blessing."

"He's also a good eater—loves left-over steak. When Luci has a dog-walking commitment, I drive her to it and walk with her. The dogs definitely prefer her. She seems to be holding her own—not depressed by the relationship between Ryan and myself."

"At first, she was angry, but she realises Ryan has reasons that we don't understand. What we do understand and live by is God's Word."

Tony made no comment. As a child his mother dressed him in his best clothes and dragged him off to Sunday School. All he learned was a few Bible verses.

Janet waved the spatula before turning her eggs, "If you only knew the wonder of God's love for you, Tony, you'd want nothing else."

Dale pushed back his chair, hastily swallowing his milk, ready to leave. Tony saluted Janet as he followed him out the door. Much later he asked Ryan, "Do you know God's love for you?"

"No. Your love is everything to me. Why do you ask? Have you been watching Robert Schuller?"

"No. It's just that happy people talk about His love for them." Tony assessed Janet's confessions in his heart. Her confidence in God and her radiant life defied reason. Perhaps God could love him, too. From time to time in his investigations he felt drawn to enter a chapel or church—but he never did.

Janet invariably told him that God loved him and indirectly

that His forgiveness would bring freedom from his lifestyle. Since Tony felt no guilt about his way of life that suggestion rolled off him like snow on a hot engine. While he wondered about feeling as close to Jesus as Janet, who said she lived in the circle of His arms, he forbade God to interfere with his life.

In his investigations he met women in broken home situations who were basket cases and whose children existed on drugs and sex, whereas Dale and Luci kept an even keel to their high school life. Furthermore, they respected and obeyed both Ryan and himself. Working with them on white water skills to fulfil their dreams of winning slaloms kept them focused and not thinking about the adults' different lifestyle.

"Ryan, perhaps we should escort the kids to church Sunday mornings. We needn't sit with them, but it would be good to share that area of their life."

Ryan scrutinized him in horror. "What on earth for? We don't need that bandaid in our lives. Aren't we happy together?"

"Of course. We're idyllic. Gosh, I don't want to miss out on a good thing. My detective mind tells me a faith-filled life is great. Look at Janet. Your rejection of her has caused her to go from strength to strength. She doesn't need you—she has Jesus."

"Yes, well! He can have her." They kissed soundly.

When Ryan was out showing a house to prospective buyers, Tony repeated his perceptions to the teenagers.

"Your mother glows so much from inner strength that people turn to watch her."

They responded with enthusiasm. "Well, she doesn't always glow around us. It's pick up your clothes; do your homework; have you walked Toby?"

"Whatever she has, if she bottled it, she'd make a fortune."

"You really think so?"

Tony nodded. Dale said, "She spends time with Mandy interceding for people and on her knees at home praying. She tells us Jesus is an alive, loving person. She knows it's difficult for us to understand but she claims someday we will. Maybe you will, too."

"No. I won't. 'Sunlight never penetrates to the deep sea currents.' In my world we see greed, corruption, hatred, stealing, murder. To me her beliefs are like Peter Pan's Never-Never Land. I take my perks where I can find them."

21

September 1985

The summer days rolled uneventfully into September. On a gloomy rainy Thursday, Tony took a break from writing reports of minor theft and assault to stretch unused muscles. From the hallway an ongoing clatter of ringing phones, humming copy machines, and clanging doors rose and fell like an abrasive symphony that matched his despair of cleaning up the overflowing clutter on his desk.

Idly staring out his window to assess the rush hour traffic, he watched a black limousine pull ahead of waiting cars. It sped away without concern for drivers who had been forced to jam on their brakes. In the resulting snarl he imagined angry faces disgruntled by the intrusion. Maybe the limousine's excuse was an emergency but he was sceptical. Regardless, he prepared to join the cacophony of horns, racing motors and pelting rain to join Ryan for a pre-dinner drink.

As he prepared to leave a phone rang repeatedly, followed by a knock on his door. Tony swivelled in his chair to glare at the burly officer striding in at this inopportune moment.

"Don't bother to say 'Come in'. We have an emergency."

"I see that you're in, Bradley. What's the trouble?"

"Sir, 911 reports a twelve-year-old girl was pulled into a black limousine by two husky men. She was walking with friends along Dupont Street on her way home from school. When the men opened the car door, they asked if the girls would like a ride home since it was raining. They refused and started to run, but the thugs grabbed Lily. Her screams caught the attention of a passer-by who called 911."

"Did the walker note the licence plate? How long ago did this happen?"

"The call just came in. We have no licence plate number. However, there can't be a large number of black limousines."

The abduction struck Tony in the gut. In the growing dusk a child being held by ruthless criminals was helpless to defend herself. Furthermore, the facts were few regarding their destination. Nevertheless, cruisers would try to find them before they disappeared into their hideout.

Tony swore with words his mother never taught him, grabbed his jacket and issued instructions. "Have you the parents' names and address? Put out an all car alert to find that limo. We'll talk to Lily's friends. They'll know her address. With men like that we must move quickly or we're too late. White slavers know how to cover their trail. Why do they prey on children? It's horrible! Come on, Bradley, let's go."

"I have the friend's phone number and address. We'll talk to her in the car."

Knowing each moment counted, they felt as if they were on a timed game show without any answers. Pre-empting a police car parked on the street, they drove to the friend's house. The girl, safely home but still in shock, described the kidnapper. Although well dressed, he had a hard face with cold, slanting, pinched eyes and balding hair. He looked like a prize fighter with squarish build, strong arms and big feet. When he reached out his arm, for a moment she and her friends were paralysed with fright, then they ran. Lily being the closest to the kerb was trapped.

Back in the cruiser Bradley and Tony checked the time. Five o'clock.

"Yeah. The 'come with me and I'll give you candy' type. I'll phone her parents to see if they have been told. If not, we'll be at their house shortly. Gun it, Brad."

With the siren blaring they manoeuvred in and out of traffic. En route Tony phoned the man's description to sergeants in the office so they could check out known paedophiles and other types that preyed on young girls. If any fitted the details they were to prepare rap sheets. He bet to himself that none of them drove a black limousine. As well he phoned the school in hopes someone still there knew if a limo had been spotted hanging around their area. Unfortunately, no one answered. Tomorrow he would try again.

The man with the strong arms had accomplices. Where had these monsters come from? Whoever they were, Lily faced mortal danger. Such men had to be evil—especially the one who masterminded this kidnapping. Such a smooth getaway told the officers the criminals had struck before without them knowing. This time, however, he knew they had to be caught before they sexually abused Lily. This little girl now stood for all children hurt by predators.

"Brad, the parents have been told. They're stunned and full of anguish. I wish we could give them hope that we'll return their daughter safely, but it's iffy. It's the worst scenario parents face. All we can tell them is that we're doing everything possible; which is true but flimsy, for the odds that we'll succeed are slim. The kidnappers are more likely to return Lily than we are to find them."

Brad answered by putting his foot down on the accelerator. At the child's home, cars lined the street on both sides. They leapt up the steps and rang the doorbell with their ID as police officers ready to show. Immediately the door opened.

A slim Filipino woman, with tears flowing down her cheeks, her black hair rolled in a bun that frayed at the edges like a fringed scarf, greeted them. "Officers, welcome. Come into the den. My ladies prayer group are arriving and already praying in the livingroom."

"What are they going to do?"

"We pray to Jesus, our Lord and Deliverer, for Lily's safe return. He is the God of miracles. You're welcome to join us, but if you have doubts you might hinder."

"From questioning Lily's friends we have a description of the kidnapper and the car. Unfortunately, no one got the licence plate. Do you know anyone who drives a black limo? We're tracking all the registered ones."

"No. I don't know any. They must be very evil men."

"Yes. Please give us a photo of your daughter and describe her."

"She is twelve years old, about four feet, slight build, Filipino with black hair, brown eyes, oval face, beginning to be pretty. She has a pleasant disposition; can be quite determined."

Taking the family photo in which a happy Lily stood with her father's arm around her, Tony studied it. He let out his breath very slowly; understanding and the beginning of fear crept into his face.

"Thank you, Mrs Puce. We'll be in touch. If you think of anything that might help us, please phone at once. Good night."

As they found their way out, two more ladies entered. The mother pointed them to the livingroom where ten other women knelt or walked praying fervently. The officers listened for a moment to the mounting hubbub, then left to search for Lily on the streets.

They pointed their cruiser towards the territory of an informant. He might know who recruited children for the sex trade—probably for another country. At Jerry the Pickpocket's door Bradley left a note in code that meant 'Come quickly to 52nd division police station. Urgent.'

Their next stop at McDonald's drive-through they picked up cheeseburgers, fries, apple pies to eat at the office while on the phones. All night they would chase leads—invisible or practical—also sending out descriptions across the country. In spite of their prompt actions, Tony worried. Once these brutes intimidated or forced Lily, she would be difficult to find. Contrary to his normal reasoning, he felt a strange sensation of comfort remembering those ladies on their knees in Lily's livingroom.

Within the hour Jerry the Pickpocket showed his face in Tony's office. Although he wore a puzzled expression, he sat as if ready to flee, causing Tony to wonder what caper he had recently successfully pulled. However, Tony didn't care; he wanted Lily safely home. To that end they made Jerry comfortable with a hot cup of tea. Jerry responded with theatrical amazement that cops could be nice. After giving him the details, they first asked about the black limo.

"Probably a rental. If not, then it's a dead end."

"Officers are checking car rental agencies. Two, possibly three men kidnapped the girl. The man described by Lily's friends has a square build, balding, a mean face with cold, slanting eyes, overpowering in appearance like the Incredible Hulk according to the girls. They may be Oriental. Lily is Filipino. Have you seen a man that fits that description?"

"If I did, I'd run the other way from those bruisers. I know the type. They're ruthless and sadistic. I hope the girl doesn't cry. Did her friends notice any tattoos or torn ears?"

"They were too upset but we'll broach them again. Possibly they'll remember more. Where does the torn ear man live—is he an ex-wrestler?"

"The pawnshop owners might have his phone number. For a while he was down on his luck and pawned personal stuff in my area. Then suddenly he was flush, wearing fancy suits, said he worked as a bodyguard."

"Okay, Jerry. Here's something for coming promptly. I don't think you want us to drop you in a police cruiser. Good night."

Pulling his cap over his eyes, Jerry left.

Brad and Tony faced each other. A few leads that had been phoned in were being checked out by other officers. Troubling thoughts filled Tony's brain. How could they face Lily's parents if they didn't find her alive? Tony felt a wrenching pity inside him like a cramp in the stomach.

"Brad, we'll check con photos to sort out ones that fit this man's category." Tony pulled at his lower lip then phoned Ryan.

"Dear, I'm starting on a new case that is urgent—a kidnapped child. It'll be a few hours before I park in our driveway."

Ryan's disappointed voice slurred his words. No concern for the kidnapped child was expressed. Tony frowned as he replaced the receiver—the encouragement he needed hadn't been forthcoming.

22

Darkness enveloped the city from the downtown core to the river's edge.

Inside Lily's home, guitar players softly strummed hymns while mothers propped up their Bibles to read verses of protection and deliverance. Calling on Jesus' name, they prayed the Word. In unity and absolute faith that God was able and that He would do what He said He would, they commanded in the authority given to them by the name of Jesus.

"Dear God, we thank You for Lily, for the joy she brings. Now she's in trouble and we're standing in faith for her safe return. Jesus, in Your name, we command those men to fall into a deep slumber—such a sound sleep that Lily will be left alone and she will find a way to escape. God, You know where she is and what she has to do. Send Your angels to free her.

"You sent angels to lead Peter out of his chains and prison. You have no favourites. We believe You are doing the same for Lily. Thank You Jesus."

After the joint prayer each woman switched into praying gear using their own language in a crescendo of emotions, yet in one accord. They punctuated their prayers with shouts of "Put those men to sleep. They shall not hurt Lily—she's God's daughter. Show her how to escape. We believe in miracles, and we ask You to send people to those men to convict them to repentance. O God You are mighty and we love You. Your ways are great and mighty to behold."

At length, they sensed His Presence among them and knew He kept His promise to make a way where there seemed no way. Lily's mother's eyes stopped brimming over; the guitarists ceased their music; in their hearts they waited. Like the prayer meeting held by St Peter's friends they planned to prevail in prayer all night. Meantime they willed prayerfully for Lily to be bold and guided to escape.

Tony, tired of studying sullen photos of known offenders, called for a squad car so he and Bradley could patrol streets where prostitutes paraded their wares. Although they showed Lily's photo to many persons, no one had seen her. After a fruitless hour, Tony said, "They've taken her to a house preparatory to spiriting her away to another city. We have to keep a surveillance out for the kidnappers."

Helplessness threatened to choke the officers' spirits. In an agony of indecision Tony studied Bradley's profile. Part of him wanted to form a posse to scour the city—door to door if necessary—to find these criminals and free the girl; while another part of him knew he could not—he had no idea where they were hiding her, nor did he know whether or not they carried guns. His instincts told him the men in the black limousine regularly conducted abductions.

Bradley swivelled to gauge Tony's reaction to a startling hunch. "If I were planning to kidnap a child, I'd do it from one of those old isolated estates on the river's banks. Most of them have been abandoned because they're so dilapidated. Why don't we try the area full of old genteel houses with their big rooms, long driveways and overgrown bushes that hide them from other isolated houses?"

"Yes!" Tony found the idea as riveting as winning a jackpot. "What a striking suggestion! Let's check it out." He swung the cruiser around to proceed to the city's northern suburb.

After the kidnapping, the driver floored the limo's accelerator, ploughing into the crowded middle lane in his headlong race to the next main intersection. At the corner he turned sharply, pouring power to the engine to swing to the right and onto the access ramp of the city's bypass highway. Speeding as if the road was a raceway, other cars frantically swerved to pull out of his path.

In the middle seat the burly man pushed a terrified screaming Lily to the floor. He then hauled a large handkerchief out of his pocket and stuffed it into her mouth to gag her. A third fellow, equally big and menacing with a torn ear, held her legs while they turned her over to bind her hands behind her back.

Big Hank warned, "If you kick any more we'll bind your legs also. Be still. You better co-operate or else." He slapped her backside.

"Okay Joe," he yelled at the stylishly clad driver, "our work here is finished. We caught us 'uns a healthy one." He grinned at his accomplice.

"Hey Joe, cool it. We don't want the coppers to stop us."

"Ah, don't worry. If they do, we'll throw a coat over her."

Lily, lying on the floor, couldn't see in what direction they drove. Extremely uncomfortable, terrorized by the overpowering men, and gagging on the handkerchief, tears streamed down her cheeks. She wanted the car to stop but dreaded what they might do to her—she was petrified into utter despair.

In the midst of rush hour, the limo man manoeuvred between lanes of traffic, barely missing speeding cars. A half hour later the right-hand signal beeped as Joe rocketed the limo onto the off ramp for an older neighbourhood.

Since he knew the city's streets as if he had designed them for a Monopoly game, he sailed along the main street with a flourish, easing off the accelerator to turn a corner two blocks up and then two blocks over. Finally he found a little-used wide lane in the once ritzy old section.

A few large old mansions, relics of *nouvelle riche* families in the 1800s, lined the narrow street's one side on which three streetlights vaguely blinked. Three estates, long abandoned and neglected, were half hidden behind unhindered growth of foliage, weeds and sky-touching trees. The first house's silhouette against the lights of the city outlined a menacing three-storey edifice that boasted a turreted cupola, steep slanted roof and at the side a portico under which passengers once descended from their vehicles. In spite of its stark loneliness, the limo continued past it.

Half a mile on, Joe cranked the steering wheel hard left, pulled onto a circular drive and braked in front of an early Georgian house. The long drive to the front door provided privacy. No one would see or hear Lily scream. She was totally at the mercy of her kidnappers.

The neglected white brick house had been built by a lumber magnate who in the Georgian style balanced its windows with imported stained glass. Etched window glass and a fan-shaped window framed the door. Neglected interior rooms contained sheet-covered furniture in the midst of rotting curtains and disintegrating walls. What were once Aubusson carpets now lay on the floor as filthy relics. The stench of decay and mould hung in the air.

Mournfully soughing fir trees increased Lily's fears that she might be killed at any moment. Hank lifted her from the car and slung her over his shoulder, carrying her into the front hall. He dropped her to the floor, then prodded her to walk ahead of him towards the rear passageway where a lighted candle feebly wavered. In the oversize kitchen, the men deposited Lily on a narrow chair while Joe lighted a propane lantern.

"Be careful with our cargo, Hank," Luigi growled. "We'll ask a good price for her from the syndicate. Untie those hands. She's too scared to cause trouble."

Lily, her eyes like those of a frightened doe, looked on the verge of fainting. But her survival instinct rose up and she willed herself to neither collapse nor to flounder in despair.

Hank grunted at the order but complied. Then he swung his swivel chair around to face the two other well-dressed men. Luigi, the leader, paced in an expensive pinstripe suit matched to fine Italian leather shoes. His more laidback partner, Joe, sported an Armani sports jacket and carefully pressed trousers. Both wore shirts of finest lawn. In contrast, Hank wore the castoffs of a thug. Luigi especially studied Lily with small, close-set eyes. Waving a fine boned, expensively manicured hand, he waited for the partners to gather for a moment.

"Let's heat some spaghetti before we carry this gal upstairs," Luigi suggested. "I don't know my way around a kitchen. You'll have to cook." He directed the order at Joe.

"Now the old gas stove's gone to the dump, I'll cook on the camp stove. If you're hungry enough you'll eat my cooking. Luigi, we'll stay here for the night, won't we? The cops'll be searching for a black limo but they won't see it here."

He opened a box on the floor from which he extracted the camping equipment.

As soon as they had eaten their spaghetti, Joe said, "Let's move into the sunroom where there are some padded chairs. Suddenly I'm feeling tired."

He walked through an archway to the sunroom, where he sprawled in an easy chair, closing his eyes.

Luigi followed him and lay back in the recliner. "Must be catching," he muttered. "I'm exhausted. That's okay. We'll be up at 4 a.m. for a long drive tomorrow."

Hank, too, slumped onto the couch thinking, 'I'll just relax for a minute.' One by one they collapsed on the furniture, chins on their chests until, each in their own key, they produced a snoring saw contest.

Lily witnessed the thugs' unusual sleep habits in amazement.. She ought to be the one who was sleepy but she was wide awake. How odd!

Not convinced that the kidnappers slept soundly, she tiptoed close to them to double-check their closed eyelids. Their faces were so ugly and mean she decided she had to escape before they carried out their evil plans.

"How can I escape? Oh Jesus, help me."

23

At the prayer meeting Lily's mother answered the doorbell, hoping to find her daughter standing there. Instead she saw Pastor Padillo and his wife holding out their arms. They hugged the broken-hearted mother, then entered the livingroom. Cries of relief were uttered that their shepherd had arrived to guide them. Quickly he knelt to join their entreaties. In size he was a sliver of a physical being but in his spirit he was a King David—a slayer of giants.

Giving the victory sign he read from Psalm 40: 1-3.

> *I waited patiently for the Lord;*
> *He turned to me and heard my cry.*
> *He lifted me out of the slimy pit,*
> *Out of the mud and mire;*
> *He set my feet on a rock.*
> *And gave me a firm place to stand.*
> *He put a new song in my mouth,*
> *A hymn of praise to our God*
> *Many will see and fear*
> *And put their trust in the Lord.*

"While travelling in India I met a man who carried in his pocket a small Bible. The book was water stained around the edges. He told me that often he fished in one of the big water tanks that contained fish for people to catch. One day he fell into

92

the deep tank, sinking down and down, for he couldn't swim. Crying out to Jesus he felt rock so solid under his feet it pushed him up to the tank's edge. Fellow fishermen who knew he couldn't swim ran in amazement to kneel before him, for they thought he must be a god. He denied that he was a god, but told them he served a powerful God who kept His word.

"We know Jesus, too. In Colossians 2: 15 the Word says, 'And having disarmed the powers and authorities, he made a public spectacle of them, triumphing over them by the cross.'

"Jesus is doing the same to these Satan-controlled men who stole your daughter. We pray in faith, Father."

Once more the hum of assertive voices filled the room, while on the dark streets police cruisers searched for the kidnapped girl.

Lily familiarized herself with the kitchen, searching for an easy escape. The windows were low enough so she could open them and jump out. However, the possibility of brambles and other lurking snares in the outside darkness made her reject that route. Instead she slipped through the slightly ajar kitchen door into the long hallway to the front door. She hoped her heart that pounded like a set of drums, deafening in its volume, could not be heard by the men.

Carefully turning the lock, opening and closing the door so it wouldn't slam shut, Lily was outside and she took to her heels. To the left a hedge and inky blackness created a void of infinite proportions; to the right a lone streetlight glowed at the junction with another street where houses appeared to be inhabited. The clouds had opened to allow a hazy moon to brighten the sky. She needed its light to avoid stumbling on irregular paving and stones in the driveway. But on the wide lane her feet flew, taking her away from danger to the house-lined street. Once she tripped on a stone but picked herself up, losing scarcely a moment's time.

Her breath came in gasps. Still she would not stop. She had to go farther. A rustling noise from the far side startled her and gave wings to her feet. Around her loomed the gloomy phantoms of tall fir trees. Turning left by the streetlight she tried to keep in the shadows. She listened; but no hurried feet followed her, so she ran on. Her chest ached, still she dared not pause to catch her breath.

On the pavement of the more populated thoroughfare she drew on a reserve of strength to run faster and faster. Houses lining the street looked to be well tended, but at this hour not many lights could be seen in them. When she could not run another step, she bent over, hands on knees, to catch her breath. She continued to shiver with fear, clinging to hope that her freedom was permanent. What should she do in case they followed her? Should she knock on the door of a house and pour out her wild story? By the time people answered the door, the thugs would have captured her.

Since she had run two blocks almost to the main road, she looked for a hiding place in which to recuperate. In the long verandah of a nearby house, she found a hopefully safe corner. Looking over her shoulder she climbed its steps and crouched in shadows by a spirea bush. She was exhausted. She hoped the men would drive by in their limo, for then she could safely find people to help her. Her father and mother's faces flashed into her mind's eye and she wished desperately to see them again.

At random Bradley and Tony exited the freeway following an avenue in a formerly wealthy district. "This street is too populated. Turn left at the next block," Tony suggested.

"Wait. Let's ask in that coffee shop. There's a number of people in it. They'd remember if they saw a black limo."

The owner looked up as they entered the restaurant. "Good evening, officers. Coffee is on the house. It's good to have unsavoury people think my place is a police hangout."

"Thanks. Cream in one. One black. Who are your unsavoury people? We're looking for a few who drive a black limo."

"I've seen the limo driving by a few times in the past week. Where it ends up I don't know. We're not the type of neighbourhood for a luxury car to be in. When I was a kid this place was prosperous, but not any more."

He looked at his regular customers. "You know this area, too. Anyone seen where the limo goes? Why do you want to know?"

"They kidnapped a 12-year-old girl late this afternoon. We need to catch them before they take her to another city."

A tall older man stifled an oath. "I've seen it. A car like that is unusual around here, so I noticed. I've seen it go over a couple of blocks and turn left onto Belmont Avenue."

Tony looked at Bradley. "What's at the end of Belmont? Is there a good hiding place where they wouldn't be disturbed?"

"You bet. On a wide lane there's the old Mayfair Mansion surrounded by land that coasts down to a creek. It's uninhabited because the heirs have quibbled over it for decades. Perfect for your criminals."

"They're not our criminals yet—but they will be. How do we find Mayfair Mansion?"

"Easy. Two blocks over turn left. Then turn right for two blocks on Johnson Street until you come to Winding Lane. Make another right and you'll spot it. Good luck."

"Thanks for the coffee and advice." Tony gave a thumbs up.

While Bradley sipped his coffee, Tony put in a call for more police cars to come to the area but to stay off Winding Lane until they checked with them. "Let's go, Brad. Oh God, I hope we save her."

When Brad drove down Johnson Street he eased off the accelerator, carefully surveying the houses. No cars or pedestrians moved on the thoroughfare. As Winding Lane appeared to be a few blocks down they veered to the kerb and stopped. The street seemed abnormally quiet. They had planned to walk; instead they decided to turn off the car lights and coast to the lane.

Lily heard the car moving slowly along the street. Oh no! They were searching for her. But the car came from the wrong direction. Peeking around the verandah's stone pillar her eyes opened wide at the sight of a police cruiser. Was it safe to go out on the sidewalk to hail them? She had to risk it. Still frightened, she crawled along the verandah to keep out of sight until she reached the steps.

A sobbing excited sound creeping along the verandah of a nearby house made the policemen freeze with their hands on pistols. But only for a few seconds. Lily rushed down the front steps into Tony's arms.

"Oh, I'm so happy to see you! I'm Lily," she gasped breathlessly. "I didn't know what to do to get somewhere safe." She cried from relief.

Tony gently picked her up and placed her in the middle of the front seat. "We're glad to see you, too. You're safe now. We'll take you home. How did you escape?"

"It was easy. The men fell asleep so I walked out and ran until I couldn't run any more. Then I hid on the verandah."

"Where is the house?"

"Go to the streetlight at the end of the street, turn right and the house is on a circular driveway on the left."

"Good girl. I'm just going to radio the information to the police cars zeroing in on this area. They'll capture the thugs, but we're taking you home to your worried parents."

Immediately he asked the dispatcher to phone Lily's parents to tell them they had found her and were bringing her safely home. He smiled as he thought how relieved they would be.

Tony didn't need to radio the other cruisers. They had arrived. After he instructed them, they surrounded the house; then ordered the kidnappers out over their loudspeaker. It took a long time because the thugs slept so soundly that finally a few officers had to enter by the unlocked front door and drag them out.

En route to their jail cells, Hank, who thought he worked with slick operators, exploded at them. "You're the freakiest bunch I've ever worked with!"

24

Brushing his hand over his brow and hair to ease his tension, Lily's father glanced into the livingroom to find his wife. She circulated among the gathering of friends scattered about the furniture in various poses—kneeling, sitting, standing as in a game of frozen tag. No longer praying intensely, they relaxed and waited.

A ringing telephone animated the group—heads turned to watch with suspended breath while Mr Puce picked up the receiver. He barely touched it as if it were a hot potato.

He answered with a reserved, "Hello." Silence. In a split second, his face became a grinning jack-o'-lantern. "Yes. Thank God. And thank you so much, officers. We'll be so relieved to have her back. You must come in when you get here."

His petite wife tugged his arm, "Who was it? What did they say?"

"Darling, she's safe! The police not only found Lily; they've captured the kidnappers. Lily is fine. She's recovering from the trauma of her ordeal and they credit her for escaping and leading them to the abductors. Thank You Jesus that our daughter is on her way home." He swept his wife up in the air and together they danced with joy.

When the police cruiser parked at the Puces' door, dancing figures in the windows twirled to songs of praise. Taking Lily's hand the two officers walked her to the wide open entrance, through which she ran into her father's and mother's arms.

Sobbing with relief, Mrs Puce immediately escorted Lily upstairs to the security of her bedroom while her father pumped the officers' hands in gratitude and Pastor Padillo, the only person who could quieten the group, announced Sunday morning service would be a thanksgiving service complete with a banquet afterwards to celebrate their Lily's safe return.

"And officers, you will be the guests of honour for finding and returning our daughter. The roasted lamb will be delicious. You must come or it will be an incomplete celebration."

Tony reeled in surprise at the impact of the words of this man who barely reached to his chin. Bradley had already agreed to attend, but not Tony. He shifted feet as he looked around at the exulting people. Inside himself Tony knew that for Lily's rescue they had outside help, supernatural help. How did these people bring about this happy ending? He realised these Filipinos relied on their God; because the usual scenario in a kidnapping case was that the child ended up on the missing persons list. Although he was grateful that Brad and he had participated in Lily's safe return, he still couldn't understand it. If he hadn't been outside Mayfair Mansion watching the half-asleep thugs captured, he would not have accepted reports of the events. Lily's escape defied all reasoning.

Towering over the toothpick thin Pastor, Tony experienced a new feeling of humility. Whatever was going on, he liked the joyous results. Their contagious laughter was lacking in his life. He thought, 'We need to lighten up more. Maybe Ryan would attend the feast with me. Perhaps the youngsters would leap at the opportunity.'

From behind her father, Lily scampered down the stairs calling, "Oh officers, please come to the feast. You've been so nice."

"I'll try to make it on Sunday," Tony grinned and poked Brad to get going.

"We're expecting you," replied Pastor Padillo.

Outside, as they walked to the car Tony said, "Brad, I didn't know you were a Christian. You're on the same wavelength as those people."

"I don't talk it but I try to walk it. If you knew how wonderful life with Christ in your heart is, you would accept it in a flash. Where depressing, black situations exist, He brings light. Remember the song, 'Because He lives, I can face tomorrow'."

"My mother took me to Sunday School," Tony recalled. "But in my teens I did what most other teenagers were doing, especially sexual exploits. I charmed my way through social happenings, even becoming bisexual. Hey! Whatever was out there, I wanted. But life isn't one big amusement park. When the thrilling ride ends, you have to find bigger excitement. The thrills wear off, leaving emptiness. Those Filipinos aren't in it for the ride—they've found a satisfying way to live. As you know, Ryan is my partner and in his love I find great fulfilment. If Ryan agrees to come, I'll attend the celebration."

"Sleep on it. Even if Ryan refuses to go, you go to the Filipino church on Sunday because you won't want to disappoint Lily—she's looking forward to you being there. Furthermore, you'll be blessed beyond expectation." Brad almost broke into holy laughter. "Good night, Tony."

Tony's mind continued to spin with thoughts of what would happen at the feast as he settled behind the steering wheel and roared the engine. His predicament was without precedent. The night's events were unbelievable. Ryan would doubt it. He'd think it an entertaining story but he wouldn't credit it as true. But Tony was stuck with the fact he'd lived through the outcome, witnessing the power of prayer. Even though he was happy Lily was safely home, he couldn't claim that the officers rescued her. It had been a stronger force than the police that kept her safe.

The hard-nosed cop knew the Filipinos' prayers couldn't have put the kidnappers to sleep. They had to be on drugs. Yet, because they did fall so soundly asleep, Lily escaped to safety with her family. He wanted to believe it was a combination of drugs and prayer. But why would they be on drugs during a kidnapping? What the hell! He couldn't make sense of these goings-on.

Still, Lily had given him such an insistent, special invitation that he didn't want her to be disappointed by the absence of her new friends. To her Brad and he were Superman and Spiderman rolled into one. It would be unkind not to let her thank them. When the backlash from her trauma hit her, she needed to know policemen care.

Tony tried and tried to file the night's events away in a suitable category. They refused to line up. Up to this evening, he had operated factually by gathering all pertinent information, then sorting it into relevant categories. All facts were explainable. But tonight's events were neither explainable nor reasonable.

Tony finally decided that although Lily was home safe and alive through miraculous but true circumstances, he would not rationalize these happenings. They needed more happy endings—more people praying.

Dragging himself out of the car, he entered their apartment. The clock struck midnight as he switched off the hall light and tiptoed into the bedroom.

"Is that you Tony? Where have you been? I missed you." Ryan snapped on the bedside light to check his partner's appearance. When he detected an unusual peace on Tony, he wondered if his fears were true. "You're out partying while I'm home after a terrible day." He sat up glaring.

Quickly shedding his clothes, Tony wearily crept onto the bed. "Did you lose out on that sale? I'm sorry. It's been a tension-filled day for me, too. A girl being kidnapped is not a laughing matter."

"Who's laughing? Did you find her?"

"Ryan, I've not been drinking. This is a believe it or not story. In late afternoon and into the evening we frantically searched for a black limousine that had kidnapped a 12-year-old Filipino girl. It was like looking for Waldo at a hunters' convention.

"We reported to her parents who were already hosting a powerful prayer meeting. The Filipinos prayed for the kidnappers to fall into a deep sleep and for Lily to find a way to escape."

"Don't try to tell me it happened!"

"Scouts' honour, that *is* what happened." Tony knew he had not hit home plate.

Ryan's eyes hardened as he listened to Tony's out-of-character story. "Oh yeah!"

"So help me Ryan, this report is too weird to make up. Because we were so concerned we carried out standard procedures. But we couldn't stop—we had to do something, so we decided to drive to an area where abandoned old estates would be suitable to hide in.

"When we drove down the street before coming to the deserted neighbourhood, the girl came running to our cruiser. It happened according to the Filipinos' prayers."

"Humph," Ryan cleared his throat. "Sheer coincidence. You're not going to believe that nonsense, are you? I've heard about it all my life and it never worked for me. Come closer. I've been lonely for you."

Stretching out beside him, Tony hesitated, "There's more. When we returned Lily to the parents' home and prayer meeting, they danced for joy."

Ryan's look of withering disdain brought Tony to a faltering coughing fit. If he didn't mention it now, he rationalized, he never would. "Pastor Padillo invited Brad and myself and families to attend their service on Sunday. Because they are celebrating Lily's safe return, they're preparing a feast for after the worship.

"He stressed that if we didn't come for the service, we'd be welcome at the feast—roast lamb, Filipino fish dishes, rice—a banquet. Lily came downstairs to give us a special invite. If that kidnapped girl had been Luci, you would celebrate with her."

"That mutt, Toby, would never allow Luci to be kidnapped. Did you say you were going?" A pulse in Ryan's throat throbbed.

"I didn't say. Brad is going and as his superior I should make an appearance. We wouldn't stay long. It would be good for the kids to share another culture's banquet."

Even as he talked, Tony knew he had to be present at the Filipino church on Sunday. He owed it to Lily, to Brad and to himself. What Ryan thought of the matter was his own affair.

Ryan turned away as if the sight of his roommate disgusted him. "Are you going?"

Tony lay in miserable silence, knowing his answer might destroy their love affair.

"These gentle people are genuine in their faith and kind generosity. They'd be disappointed and hurt if we did not share their happiness. The police chief will endorse it as great public relations, maybe give me a promotion. However, that isn't my reason for going. I want to show respect for their happiness.

"With or without you I'm going."

25

Despite Tony's brave words, doubts that in the morning crowded his mind about attending the Filipino service were reinforced by his sweetheart's ominous absence. He turned his head slowly; he knew Ryan's side of the bed was empty.

A growing uneasiness crept over Tony. Ryan had given him a final decree. After a long day of politely conversing with prospective buyers, he would not be in an amenable frame of mind. Instead of talking, he'd watch NHL hockey.

Tony paced the bedroom floor, unsettled because his thoughts chased each other in a vain hope that Ryan would soften his stance. He shoved his legs into his jeans and wrapped himself in a favourite old plaid shirt. Although his relationship with Ryan had progressed smoothly, they focused entirely on the present as if tomorrow would never arrive.

Previously, he had agreed with Ryan when he lamented Janet's obsession with church attendance. But surely, going to one church service was no cause for alarm. Still Ryan's anger left an uncomfortable knot in the pit of Tony's stomach. What caused Ryan's negative possessiveness? It wasn't jealousy—it was something his mind hovered around but couldn't pinpoint.

Slumping on the side of the bed, he rested his arms on his knees, scowling toward the window. Life no longer was painted in black and white. Although he wanted to rationalize his decisions, he couldn't until he tested them on someone else.

His alarm clock rang. Nine o'clock. The teenagers and Toby

would descend on them any moment. Where was Ryan? He wanted to play up the celebration scheduled for the next day. Maybe if Ryan made a good sale, he would be in good humour and willing to celebrate. Tony smiled; he'd bribe the kids if he had to to gain their support. Janet would be pleased they were attending.

'JANET', his inner voice shouted. He could talk to her about his experience. Tony abruptly sprang to his feet, rushed to the front door to stop her from leaving when she dropped the teenagers off. As he opened the door her car pulled up, emptying out Dale, Luci and Toby who responded, 'Uh-huh' to her last minute instructions.

"JANET," he yelled, "you must join me for a cup of coffee. A strange experience has affected me. Please come in."

A startled Janet turned off the car engine, giving the kids a what-have-you-been-up-to look. They looked as innocent as they could—equally unaware of what had come over Tony. Toby, however, knew his duty, for he walked ahead clearing the path of any possible unknowns.

In the kitchen Janet shed her jacket while Tony bustled around warming muffins and coffee. He silently thanked their cleaning lady for leaving the kitchen immaculately clean.

"Thank you for joining me, Janet. Ryan has a business breakfast. The kids are watching TV so I can talk. You're the one person who can make sense of my experience."

"I'm flattered, but I don't like talking behind Ryan's back."

"We're not talking about Ryan. I've had an inexplicable experience. I've had it so I can't deny it. It's so out of the ordinary it's mystifying. Even more amazing—I don't want to deny it happened."

"For goodness sakes, Tony, what are you talking about?" Janet's body tensed as if she were a gopher smelling danger. She wondered if he expected her to referee a quarrel between him and her ex-husband. No way. Hell would freeze over before she did that. She grasped her mug in a crushing grip. "So, Tony, what shook you up?"

Tony took a deep breath and grinned. "This week I witnessed the faith that moves mountains. A twelve-year-old Filipino girl was kidnapped in broad daylight as she walked with her friends on her way home from school. We went into high gear searching for the black limousine that abducted her—without any results. However, her parents and friends prayed relentlessly. Janet, they prayed for the kidnappers to fall asleep and for Lily to be shown how to escape. And it happened. It was completely unpredictable. We were drawn to the area where Lily was waiting for us and drove her home. Inside that house was the presence of God. I felt so wonderful—I hated to leave. It made me realise how selfish my actions have been. Janet, I'm truly sorry I acted as though you didn't exist and broke up your home. If you can, please forgive me."

Janet's eyes gleamed kindly, "Tony, I forgave you months ago. Unless we know God, we act selfishly; even now I unintentionally do. I've prayed for you to know God's love. Until you have the revelation of God's love, you don't know what it is to be really loved. You've tasted it. There is more. Pursue Him to gain the fullness of His love, that is Christ in you. When He shows you how great He is, He's showing how much He wants you. The more you open up to His love—the more everything will fall into place. Don't wait."

Tony blinked away unshed tears. While his brain cleared, Janet held his hand, beaming God's love into him. "I'm impressed by the powerful prayers of the Filipino church. Did they tell you the reason for their absolute trust in God's faithfulness?"

"Yes. Pastor Padillo and other members have had relatives in the Philippines killed because they talked about the glory of Jesus. Mrs Puce's brother was martyred when he was only fifteen years old."

"No wonder they are so committed and move mountains."

"Bradley, my partner, and I are invited to the Filipino Church service followed by their celebration for Lily's safe return. Since Ryan isn't interested, I doubt that he'll go, but the youngsters would enjoy it. May I take them?"

"I've always trusted you with them. But you'll have to ask the kids. I think it'd be a broadening, great experience. And if there's an altar call run to the front to receive Jesus. It will be the best step you ever took. God provides an alternative that brings people out of bondage. And He's there for you, too."

During commercials, Dale raced into the kitchen to nab potato chips. He gulped when he saw Tony's wet eyes; he was a hardened detective. Something awful must have happened. Then he looked at his mother's joyous face and decided it was too complicated. Janet walked with him to the livingroom. "I hope you two go to service with Tony tomorrow morning. Bye." Dale knew she smiled all the way to the car.

She still smiled when she parked in Mandy's driveway. Surprisingly she found her friend alone. "Kids have gone to friends. Jack's working in the basement. You look mighty pleased. What's up?"

Janet told Mandy about Tony's contact with Spirit-filled Christians that left him struggling to understand their faith. Furthermore, he planned to attend their church service on Sunday.

"Let's adjourn to the prayer room to pray his salvation through for tomorrow. No demon in hell can stop someone coming to Christ when they want to." She slanted her head to study Janet. "Someday Ryan will come, too. We'll be like those Filipino ladies—we'll pray till Jesus returns. Oh Hallelujah!"

Taking prayer positions as determined as soldiers in battle, they reminded God of His promises. Standing on His Word they claimed full salvation for Tony at the Sunday service. They prayed until they were flooded with the peace that transcends understanding.

On Sunday morning Toby, resplendent in his new plaid coat, trotted into the livingroom with Luci. Going to Ryan, who lounged in his velvet housecoat in front of the fireplace, Toby waited patiently for pats on his head, then lay at Ryan's feet.

106

"Toby is rather friendly this morning." Ryan looked over his reading glasses at Luci who was rescuing the comics from Dale.

"Oh Daddy, he thinks you're lonely without him on your lap or at your feet. Maybe he likes your scent." In a moment of budding woman's intuition she sensed her father's loneliness even with his children and lover around him. Bravely she asked, "Are you coming with us to the Filipino service Tony is so hyped about?"

"No. No I'm quite tired this morning. You two go with him. Toby'll keep me company."

"If I leave Toby with you, you'll fatten him with treats. I'm going to stay with you. You're usually with one of the males. Now I can have you all to myself." She looked smug as she joined Toby at his feet.

Ryan ruffled her hair. He was startled to realise that she was half grown and he didn't want to lose her for another few years. Still, he knew her presence wouldn't make his loneliness disappear—maybe nothing could.

"Your mother expects you to go with Dale and Tony. She'll want an accurate report. Toby, I'll not part with. He keeps my feet warm. Only if he rolls over and plays dead will I give him a treat."

"Promise," Luci was not sure about the arrangement.

Ryan did not promise. However, Luci managed to leave the apartment without Toby at her heels. Sprawling in the car's back seat, she wished she knew someone at this strange church.

In the front seat, Tony described a few people who impressed him at the prayer meeting. Mostly he elaborated on details of the feast that was to follow the final hymn. He became so enthused about the good Filipino cooking, they couldn't find the building in which the service was held. All the description of roasted lamb and side dishes created an appetite in them and now they were lost.

Finally, Tony stopped at a gas station, where the attendant showed him the location on a map. "We're near it. Hang on. I'll get us there on time."

They hung on until he whipped the car into the parking lot. Dale teased, "I don't smell roast lamb. It can't be the right place."

Tony pretended to cuff him. "Get out of the car. We've found the church."

After rushing up an outside staircase of a three-storey building to a long second floor balcony, the trio stumbled on the Filipino Church. In the first doorway they surprised a small group of people who for a few minutes exchanged pleasantries and warm greetings. After their ears adjusted to the music blaring from the front, they excused themselves to find the pastor.

A row of windows on the left sent light bouncing off cream painted walls. Porcelain vases filled with fragrant cut flowers intermingled with band instruments and overflowed into side aisles. An indeterminate number of children checked their family seating location before obeying farsighted mothers to run off energy by visiting first floor rest rooms.

In the adjacent hall, they passed rooms used for Sunday School and a kitchen. They paused, intrigued by tantalizing smells of sweet well cooked lamb, aromatic spices used in sauces and pungent ginger and garlic in vegetables. Cooks held wooden spoons to lips of grandmothers to check that no ingredient had been missed. Hungry husbands who also offered their taste buds in hopes of a sampling were shooed away.

Dale and Luci stayed close to Tony, unsure of their surroundings and the happy, friendly faces. Soon Mrs Padillo welcomed them, delighted to see Luci and Dale, whom she assured would be taken care of by their teenagers. As she escorted them into the worship centre, she explained that the front row was reserved for some elderly members, even though they were not always able to attend. Thus the second row became the place of honour. Already seated there a grinning Bradley and his family shifted over to give them empty chairs.

Tony's detecting eye noted nothing unusual in the setup of padded folding chairs in rows, a podium at the front that he could almost touch. Behind it, drums, electronic piano and guitars along with seats for the youth group choir filled the front space. The ensemble equipment gave him hope that the music would be good and lively.

Behind them a few people sat in chairs but most of them walked about chatting or reading notices on the bulletin board. Mothers raised their voices at excited offspring. Fathers gestured wildly as they punctuated their argument with friends. If he hadn't known it was a church service, he would have called it a gathering for a large family. Not at all what he expected.

Then Pastor Padillo and his assistant stepped to the front, smiled broadly at the officers, and quoted a psalm, the Call to Worship. Miraculously every person settled themselves; the musicians glued themselves to their instruments and the choir poised themselves by their chairs opposite the drums. The ordinary artefacts were transformed.

Tony regarded the fiery pastor with surprise. Beside him Dale looked uncomfortable; Luci chewed gum while her thoughts wandered elsewhere. From the corners of their eyes, the teenage choir studied them warily until one girl smiled in their direction. After that they broke into undefined groups of interest with each other while the pastor spoke. Behind Tony children scuffled; one dropped his collection dime and was admonished by his mother; at the back a baby cried. Gradually a delicious aroma of roast lamb and spicy vegetables wafted into their nostrils. Tony's stomach constricted in hunger.

Yet the words from the Bible penetrated Tony's hard shell of sophistication. The beautiful holiness of the praying women on the previous week began to manifest in the present assembly. The pastor quoted John 3:16. God's love surpassed any earthly love—even that of a mother. God so longed to have His love returned by His children that He sent His only Son to take our sins and punishments upon Himself so we could go free. Pastor Padillo walked to the aisle proclaiming: "It is the great exchange—all our misery and mistakes we give to Him so He can give us eternal life. How did He do it?

"God paid the ransom with Jesus' blood so that every person

who wants to shake off their chains of bondage will go free. The ransom price has been paid by Jesus dying on that cross.

"Check your consciences. 'We have all sinned and like sheep gone astray'. Everyone has. But God always makes a way out. Come, lay your burdens at the foot of His cross and you'll be reborn into the Kingdom of God—a new creation.

"Don't wait. Make your eternal life a surety. Come and we'll pray."

Around Tony swirled the congregation's normal activities. Around Tony the clouds broke—he saw a new dimension, a revelation of Jesus standing at the front with His hands outstretched. He didn't see Him with his physical eyes, but he knew the love of Jesus was drawing Tony Moretti with a monumental force. With life-or-death haste, almost running he stepped between the chairs in front of him, mounted three steps and knelt in tears at His feet.

He saw the darkness in his life—the sordidness, unpleasantness to which he could not return. Jesus, whom he saw in Janet and the praying mothers called to him, putting His hand on his head. The pure, unselfish love of God broke him—he wept, repented and fell in love with His Saviour. If he had to describe Him, he couldn't; but he knew Him. Now He was a part of him. He was no longer the same man who walked up those steps—he was a different man, a new creation. Jesus loved him and set him free.

Tony under the Holy Spirit prayers of the pastor and elders felt his body shaking until chains caused by sinful mistakes dropped off him. Then the Spirit of Love—the Holy Spirit—infilled that space, making him feel so light and clean that his joy overflowed. While the children feasted on Filipino delicacies, Pastor Padillo counselled him and gave him another pastor's name to contact. Formerly this minister had been gay but was set free by Christ. Now, he maintained a support group for sexually troubled people.

"You must contact him at once and join the meetings. The enemy is a roaring lion waiting his chance to devour you. Don't allow him to steal your salvation—your eternal life. Buy a Bible to read every day. Attend a church where Jesus is alive so you can fellowship with Him and His people. Tell one person each week what Jesus has done for you and bring them to the Lord. There are many empty spaces at His table."

Tony stood with a glowing countenance, shook the pastor's hand and thanked him. But Pastor Padillo shook his head, "Not me—it's the divine mercy of God and the prayers of all those who have prayed for you. Let's see if they left us any portions of roasted lamb."

In the next room, a somewhat reticent Dale was waited on by three girls, each vying for his attention. If he ate food served by one girl, he also had to eat what the other two brought. When one dish caused steam to come from his ears, he stood up wanting to dunk his head in a pail of water. Hastily a girl gave him a banana to cancel the burning sensation. Finally, he told them the food was delicious but he could not eat another bite.

Nearby, friendly, muscular young men towered over Luci, barely leaving room for her to move her arms. They diligently filled her plate with amazing delicacies so delicious she wanted the recipe for her mother. The weight-lifters rolled their eyes; cooking wasn't part of their desired image!

Eventually Tony, carrying an oversize plate of food wandered in to sit with Bradley and those around him. Relieved to see Tony, Dale and Luci thanked their new friends and skittered over to sit with him. Receiving their 'we want to leave' signals, he downed the food quickly so they could depart.

Driving back to the apartment, the teenagers expressed warm admiration for Tony's decision for Christ. "You don't sit on the fence," Dale observed. "You went for it full out. Congratulations."

This new, different Tony, whose face no longer froze in hard ridges to intimidate criminals, astounded Luci. She blinked her eyes to make certain they focused correctly on this face which held a new attractiveness from the Spirit's touch. Lacking appropriate words she resorted to being a little mother, "Tony, the ladies gave me two doggie bags—one for you and one for Dad."

Tony smiled, but then he couldn't stop smiling. "That's great, Luci."

He thought, 'I'm amazed that I've had a personal encounter with Jesus. It was always something floating out there that happened to "Sunday go to Meeting" Christians—not to Anthony Moretti. The last time I entered a church was for a policeman's funeral. Something inside me snapped today releasing the hold sin had on me. For once, I grasped the truth of the Bible. I feel so light and clean inside. It's beyond words. How did it happen? How blind I've been to not realise God had His hand on me. Janet's forgiveness spoke to my heart but I refused to feel any remorse. Still she spoke to my soul indirectly, forcing me to open my darkened eyes and to accept the truth of God's greater plan for my life. God loves me and I love Him. I've made a 180 degree turn to build a new life. Oh God I hope You and I can convince Ryan to accept Jesus as a living person. It will be touch and go for him to accept what I tell him. To accept Jesus means changing his lifestyle. Will he react violently? The Tony who loved him and whom he loved has been transformed. To tell him now about the love of God would inflame him.' "Boy!" he said aloud, "The outcome will be touch and go."

Everything inside him stilled, then shifted as he realised Ryan still crawled in the depths while he danced on a mountaintop.

Beside him Dale cringed, anticipating a storm. "Dad isn't going to like this."

26

Outside the car, a fierce wind swayed branches to the breaking point and impeded the teenagers' race into the apartment to collect their belongings. Ryan, who watched the football game, sat up on the couch.

"What's all the excitement? Why are you leaving so early? Did you overeat at the feast?"

"Oh Daddy, the food was delicious and we had so much attention we felt like a rock under a microscope. But it was fun."

"Where's Tony?"

Dale returned with his travel bag, giving Luci a big brother stare to get hers.

"Tony's waiting in the car. He thinks the strong wind means a storm is coming so he's taking us home now." He did not add that Tony preferred them to be absent when he talked to Ryan.

"Did something happen at this gala?"

"Yes." He edged Luci towards the door. Taking a deep breath he soldiered on, "Dad, at the close of the service, the pastor gave a powerful altar call and Tony went forward. He'll tell you about it. The transformation was amazing. He went one person but left entirely different—so happy."

"Don't tell me that crap. Not Tony—he's a hard-bitten cop who has seen all the dirty side of life. Besides, he's my lover. I know he loves me."

Luci, not to be left out, came back and hugged her father, "Well he loves Jesus now, too."

113

With a muttered oath Ryan glared. "Not possible."

Tony honked the car horn. They said, "Bye, Dad," grabbed Toby and left for their ride.

As they slammed the car door, Tony asked, "Is your dad there?"

"Yes. Dale blurted out that you met Jesus. I've never seen him so upset. Will he be alright?"

"I wish I could say 'Yes' but truthfully I don't know."

"I left my Bible in the bedroom for you," Luci said.

"Thank you. I'll read it." He patted Dale's arm, "Don't worry. He had to know and you saved me from seeing the initial shock. We'll have to trust Jesus." But why was he so worried?

Ryan stood in the livingroom, staring out the picture window. Black clouds obscured the sun, and from the gusts of chill wind tossing leaves and papers around, he judged a severe storm was imminent. He swirled his whiskey slowly, then tilted back his head to drain the glass. He couldn't bear to believe the report the youngsters had told him.

Tony held the storm door so the wind couldn't rip it out of his hands when he came in.

"Dale told me a story which I refused to believe. It didn't sound like my ardent lover. He said you gave your heart to Jesus—now that's good for a laugh."

Tony looked into serious grey eyes. "I'm not laughing; I'm in earnest. It was the most extraordinary experience—a revelation that's impossible to put into words. You have to experience it for yourself. Jesus' love is beyond anything I've ever known."

Ryan was speechless. Then the anger and hurt showed in his eyes. Their eyes held, grey eyes flashing with unwavering resistance and azure eyes darkening to midnight-blue with unyielding resolve.

"Come off your pedestal, Tony. You're as big a bounder as I am and just as selfish. You persuaded me to leave my family. Now you're saying you've got Jesus. Where does that leave me? Are you going to live your present lifestyle—with Jesus? I think not." An angry flush darkened his features.

Tony swallowed hard, thinking desperately as he ran a hand through his hair. "I wanted you to live with me thinking we had a forever love. I don't deny it, but I didn't twist your arm. You had already proposed the idea which rooted in us and caused this painful malfunction in our lives. It isn't easy for me to give you up, to hurt you and end our affair. It's as if I'm being ripped down the middle."

Ryan strode to the kitchen to pour another drink. Tony talked rapidly. "In that noisy Filipino church, a force pushed me to the front where the old Tony, dead in sin, left and a new Tony came alive in Jesus. Ryan, what we called religious nonsense is true, real, glorious. I'm alive now. Before, I wasn't. To have Jesus is where it's at."

Tony bowed his head partly from guilt and partly from still caring for Ryan not as a lover, only as a brother, who needed help. His essential nature had changed as a result of his spiritual rebirth, and that nature now demanded a lifestyle very different—a faith walk in Jesus.

Ryan whirled on him, eyes blazing with scorn. "You've had a spell fixed on you. You're deceived. We work hard. We make our jollies with deeper commitment than most gays, primarily in lust but it's been good. Now you talk Jesus' love as the only real love." He sneered, "Why do I bother listening to you? You believe that claptrap? You're an idiot."

"Yes. What can I say? I'm a crazy Christian." Ryan's bitter words tore at his defences. "My sudden new birth is a shock, I know it. But Ryan, can't you find it in your heart to forgive me, to understand my unexpected dilemma? Can't you at least try to make allowances for my new state of mind, for a wonderful, surprising blessing?"

Tony gazed at the fuming, hurting Ryan, his calm increasing as Ryan raged. He sensed the black wall of misery and despair that blocked Ryan from hearing life-giving words. He saw where unlicensed sin took a person: to a life of bitterness and regret. He sorrowed that Ryan's thinking, twisted by a transient's abuse, left him bereft of self-approval and joy. Dear God, surely you can free him.

"Make allowances? When I think of what I went through ending my family life, uprooting my children. When I think of promises of love and of living together, I realise I've been a blind fool. Did you give a thought to my wretchedness when you spurned me by going to that pastor's meeting?" He emptied his whiskey glass in one quick swallow. He dragged the bedroom door open, then slammed it behind him.

Tony couldn't blame Ryan for denouncing him. Could he desert his lover in his pain? Knowing God's forgiveness and love, would he maintain his relationship and walk in Jesus' ways? Ryan understood him; no wonder he couldn't accept this transformation. Before, he'd have thrown a fit of anger to bring Ryan into line. But no tantrum was so powerful it could heal their pain. He knew he walked a tightrope. If he fell off it into his old life he was doomed. But he chose Jesus. No, Jesus had chosen him and he loved Him with his spirit, body and soul.

He was off that island on which he and Ryan lived. Because he had escaped he would try to rescue Ryan, too. But would he co-operate?

The now weeping Ryan reopened the bedroom door to throw all Tony's belongings into the hall. "Get out of my sight. Be out of here by tomorrow morning. Go away and leave me at least to solitude, if not to peace. When I spot you at a gay club, I'll taunt you and make your name a joke," Ryan hissed.

With his head down, Tony picked up some of the artefacts of a former life, and carried them into Luci's bedroom. Immediately he spotted her Bible. Scooping it up, he switched on a reading light and settled into a reclining chair to read where the book had opened at Luke 9. He read under the subheading: 'The Cost of Following Jesus' in verses 57-62. The last verse transfixed him:

Jesus replied, *"No one who puts his hand to the plough and looks back is fit for service in the kingdom of God."*

Tony felt an invisible hand on his shoulder. "Oh Jesus, I know that only by Your grace can I be faithful. But I've been told Your grace is sufficient for me and that it comes when needed. I'm unable to cope on my own, Jesus. My flesh craves to crawl into bed with Ryan but my spirit says 'No'."

God heard and His love flowed over Tony in waves until he slept.

27

Weather meant nothing to Gramps driving his rattling truck along the highway into town to spend Sunday afternoon with Janet and the children. The strong wind and pounding rain made his old truck noisier than usual. However, the storm, as always, would blow itself out. If he arrived earlier than the appointed time of three o'clock, he hoped to chat up Janet on their current situation. Talking over the telephone was not the same as seeing the whites of their eyes or facial expressions.

If Wifey still lived, she would know the state of affairs immediately. Without her he drove to town to draw his own conclusions. The family's bad habit of trying not to upset him annoyed him immensely. 'Dratted young'uns think they know what they're doing.' He reached for his pipe to comfort himself. At their house the rain abated, allowing him to let himself in the back door.

As he shed his windbreaker, he was surrounded by smells of meat and onions, the acute waft of nutmeg on carrots, the creamy smoothness of chocolate cake. Janet was a champion baker.

"Gramps!" She was startled at his early arrival but pleased he came in spite of the storm.

"I was hoping to see you alone. I trust I'm not interrupting."

"Not at all. I'll plug in the kettle for a good cuppa. With that rattletrap you drive, I wonder how you get here. How are you?"

"With Ryan's departure, I worry lest you and the children need something or have a hurdle you need to overcome."

Janet halted her brisk, purposeful movements and held her head high. She wore a plain blue dress with a Peter Pan collar softened by a feminine touch of lace. He detected no roar of emotion in her that he felt in himself. She seemed as happy as he wanted her to be. Forcing a smile he hoped he had not overstepped his privileges. If he stopped being Gramps, they would both hate it.

"Thank you Gramps. You've always been kindness itself. We're fine. The teenagers, because they work, have learned to value their money. I earn a good salary and passed the last subject I needed in order to apply for a vice-principalship. That doesn't mean I'll get that position, but I can reapply."

Maintaining the children's well-being was a shared common cause. How she felt about his son, he wisely refrained from asking.

She looked at him with utter frankness, all the old friendship warm in her eyes, and suddenly he knew whatever else happened she would cope with dignity.

Then two overjoyed whirlwinds erupted into the room to hug their grandfather.

Surprised for the second time in half an hour, Janet said, "You're back early. Did you enjoy the Filipino service?"

Both adults listened in amazement as the teenagers recounted the episodes at the church. Luci embellished her story more than Dale had, including Tony's dash through the chairs and up the steps. In spite of Mandy and herself praying in faith, Janet's first reaction had been surprise and disbelief. The children's assertions that he really completely changed rendered her speechless.

Now that her own faith was kick-started, her joy knew no bounds. After the trauma of heartbreak, God was bringing good out of this impossible game plan. Tony, though, had seemed the least likely of the two lovers to be receptive to the Good News. Never mind, his complete turnaround would start chain reactions akin to the splitting of the atom. She hoped Ryan had adapted to the new development.

Gramps absorbed the news like the soldier he was—unperturbed but concerned for his son. "Was your dad put out over Tony's unexpected conversion?"

Dale answered, "Tony brought us home before he confronted Dad. On our way out the door we blurted it out. I think Dad was stunned—not wanting to believe it."

Gramps pulled out his pipe, cleaned and refilled it. Puffing hard on it, he had little to say. After dinner, Janet packed the leftovers in storage boxes for him to take home. Hugging Janet and kissing his grandchildren, he left undecided as to whether to visit Ryan. Since Tony was probably still at the apartment, he decided to return to the farm where life was less complicated.

*　*　*　*　*

Opening his eyes when a heavy truck ground down the street, Tony realised that he had slept dreamlessly and soundly. He rose up to check the time—seven o'clock. He knew he had to move, for all the articles and clothing still in the hallway prevented Ryan from opening his door. Time to pack it into his car. Even if he was late for work he'd clear his stuff out, lest Ryan locked him out later or threw his belongings in the garbage. 'If my conversion had been gradual Ryan might have accepted it.' Actually the experience lifted him up, while the shock of it left Ryan like a fish gasping for oxygen on dry land.

He wished they parted on friendly terms, for they had shared good times white water canoeing as well as helpping to keep up to the youngsters. Would he be able to manage with them now? Would Ryan even talk to him or would he cut him out of his life completely? He grabbed an apple from the refrigerator and munched on it intermittently while carrying load after load of clothes and articles to his car until he couldn't even squeeze in a shoelace. Sitting in the only space left, behind the steering wheel, he didn't turn the ignition key.

Chewing on his lower lip, he worried for a few minutes. He reached a decision and went back into the apartment to find pen and paper to write that he hoped Ryan would call him at the office. He propped the note on the table. Before he could change his mind he raced out to his loaded car.

Dale, slumping in his desk at high school, twiddled his pen. During dinner the previous evening, he discussed Ryan's reaction to Tony's conversion with Gramps. He felt his son would neither cope nor adjust well to Tony's new life, for it doomed their relationship. Hence, Ryan would deny the experience's validity partly because he couldn't see or touch it, and partly because he did not want to change his lifestyle.

Gramps mourned inability to change.

"What will happen to Dad? Will he come back to us?"

"I don't know. God gave us free will. It's your dad's choice. We'll continue to love him and pray for him—he can't stop us doing that. I hope you continue to visit him."

"That's a drag. Sometimes he showers us with attention; other times he's in his fantasy world or at the real estate office. But he's the only dad I have."

"Good for you, Dale. You'll be alright."

The bell rang, breaking Dale's reverie. Picking up his books he started down the hallway to his next class. He sauntered past a few hives of gossiping students. At the last group a hand reached out to grab his arm.

Anna pranced beside him to keep up with his strides. "I've been waiting to see you."

Dale grinned, "I'm glad to see you." He meant it. Looking into her clear grey eyes that darkened with concern, he relaxed slowly as if he saw a light at the end of a long tunnel. She was a touch of sanity in his emotionally racked life.

"My youth group, instead of holding a Hallowe'en party, are having a box social on the third Friday of November. Because it would be too cold to hold a carwash fund raiser, our youth minister talked us into a box social. The girls bring a delicious box lunch for the boys to bid on in an auction. You won't know

121

whose box you're bidding on but you eat lunch with the girl whose box you won. It creates a lot of suspense."

"That sounds cool, but I don't belong to your youth group."

"Dale, I'm inviting you to come as my date and hopefully to win my box lunch. We watch a movie first, then bite our nails while the boys bid. Do come."

"My grandfather took me to an auction one time. I think I'd enjoy that."

"Does that mean you will come with me?"

"Read my lips. Yes."

Anna chuckled. "Who knows? Maybe we'll eat together." Quickly squeezing his arm, she hurried to her classroom. "It's the third Friday. See you."

Dale watched her lithe figure weave in and out down the hall. As he entered his history class, he wondered what this invite meant. Kind, pretty, feisty Anna could have her pick of any male in the school. And he liked her more and more. When she was on his mind, he thought less about his father. He was a mess, but Gramps said they had to stick by him. It was hard, because Ryan's lifestyle made Dale so uncomfortable.

28

Meanwhile Tony debated whether to rent a motel room and unload his car or visit Bradley to dump his belongings in his basement. 'A friend like Brad would help me.' Also, he'd not be surprised that he and Ryan had parted ways. Bearing down on the accelerator because of the excessive weight, he headed into traffic to Bradley's house. Fifteen minutes later Brad's cheerful wife Lucille showed him where to deposit his load so it would be safe from their inquisitive children. He hugged her gratefully for the kindness before ploughing into the stream of cars to report for work.

He ignored his lateness, greeted the sergeant at the front desk and hurried down the hall to his end office to attune to strains of humming photocopiers and jangling telephones. Through a few open doors he glanced at uniformed policemen poking their computer keyboards with two index fingers. Because the work routine operated as usual, its normalcy balanced his existence. Only he and his personal life had changed.

Tony was happy to see his partner sitting by his desk. Shutting the door he said, "You see before you a homeless man."

"I know. Lucille phoned me after you left our home. Do you need a place to stay?"

"Yes, but I'm renting a motel room in order to come and go without bothering anyone. On the way here I decided I'd find a church to attend and then locate near my place of worship. Since I've never been interested before I'm at a loss to know where to start."

"I'm glad you asked, because I have the name of one which I planned to give you. Do you want it?" Brad held it high as if to make Tony jump for it.

"Cut the theatrics. Yes."

"Hickory Hills Christian Fellowship at the corner of Main Street and Hillside has a pastor named Bob Jones. He has had a few problems in his own life that he struggled with and overcame. This helped him to become a true shepherd for his flock. The living Jesus is in his growing church of newborn Christians hungry to know Jesus better and to see signs and wonders. As well he sets up classes for new converts to learn the basics of Christian living and beliefs."

"Thanks, Brad. I'll attend there next Sunday. It's amazing but all my old passions are gone. I'm hungry for spiritual food and growth."

"Be careful. Satan will try to trap you again in your old passions. Check every activity lest it leads to a temptation. Start devouring the Word. Do you have a Bible?"

"Yes. An angel named Luci gave me hers. It's neatly underlined with interesting handwritten notes in the borders. Just what I need."

29

Beginning of October, 1985

His pilgrimage began the following Sunday. Parking opposite
the Hickory Hills Christian Fellowship church to view the solidly
constructed building, Tony's eyes swept up its tower's four tall
supports to a cross encircled with a crown of thorns. In former
days the tower might have held a bell or chimes to appeal to the
ears, whereas the present artwork conveyed a vision of majesty.

Tony, following his detective pattern, pondered the tower's
symbolism briefly, before noting the wide inviting front doors, a
few stained glass windows and a parking lot already jammed with
cars. A few stragglers from the first service were getting into
their autos so new arrivals could safely park. Children hippety-
hopped through the open doors as though into Disney World.

In the crowded lobby, he threaded his way through the
multitude to an usher who headed him to the main aisle in the
nave. Among the people clustered in the pews, he easily found a
front spot. As he waited, others flowed in bringing an expectancy
that charged the atmosphere. His spirit caught the excitement.

Following the service Tony drifted into a room where
seminars often were held and where worshippers gathered for a
coffee hour to greet others and to collect offspring. While he was
hovering over the cookie table with two other males, Pastor Bob
approached him holding out his hand. His eyes, magnified by his
glasses, beamed at him. His square set body defied anyone to

tackle him physically; on the other hand, his kind expression drew people to him.

"I'm Pastor Bob and I would like to welcome you personally to our House of Worship."

"My name is Tony Moretti and I like being here. As a new convert I'm seeking every opportunity to be in this group."

After their discussion, Tony decided to attend the Tuesday evening prayer meeting. Here he placed Ryan's name on the prayer list. Wednesday he rushed to the Bible Study carrying Luci's Bible, a bit late because of an onslaught of work. He was enthralled by God's mercy—that when he repented God wiped clean Tony's page in the Book of Life. He pondered, 'If I say, "Hello God, I'm that homosexual that cursed You on June 10th", He checks the page and answers, "I don't know what you're talking about. That page is blank. You are my covenant son whom I adore and bless."'

For Tony the magnitude of God's love was awesome. Since he was a covenant son, what did 'covenant' mean? As a new Christian he had to study the Bible to learn all the important buzz- words that he didn't understand. He also had to keep close to Jesus by having fellowship with Christians who insisted his thinking patterns would change as he renewed his mind in the Word. He was learning not to underestimate Satan's wiles.

Friday he rose early to attend the men's weekly breakfast club. At the previous groups he had merely listened, but this time chomping down fried eggs and bacon, he talked. These business-men kept Bibles open beside them to confirm statements and to gain wisdom on a puzzling passage. Sexuality invariably came up. Pastor Bob reiterated that all sexual problems have their root in Satan, the Tormentor. Everyone has sexual problems to grapple with one time or another. But in Jesus we overcome these temptations and in prevailing over them we become stronger. Tony told them he slipped into homosexuality not knowing the consequences, and once in quicksand it's difficult to pull yourself out. Amazingly, Jesus did it for him. In one major operation, he had been set free of the homosexual spirit, drinking, swearing, any vice displeasing to God. All gone.

Jack, debonair and a former airline pilot, said, "I know you're very grateful. Remember to thank Him hourly until any latent temptation to backtrack is gone. Claim His protection from any traps the devil sets for you. With your hand in the hand of Jesus you'll be great. Welcome to our breakfast club. We'll pray for you—you pray for us."

"That's important," interjected Pastor Bob. "If one of us comes to mind during the day, say a brief prayer to Jesus for him. Okay men, you're going with God to your worldly outposts."

30

Half an hour later, coffee cup in hand, a whistling Tony returned to his office outpost, causing fellow workers to wonder what shaving cream he used in the morning to wake himself up. But Tony's day turned into one of the worst in his life.

Picking up his blaring emergency phone, he said, "Yep. Okay we're on our way."

Bradley appeared immediately. "I've all the names of all the residents in the Park Plaza Apartment building where the murder was committed. A young man—eighteen years old—was drowned in the bathtub."

"Then no way was it an accident. Let's go. There must be fresh clues still there."

In the apartment police were already photographing and dusting for fingerprints. All seemed in order in the livingroom, but in the bedroom suite where the corpse lay, Tony staggered, overwhelmed. Large panels covered with pictures of naked men indulging in weird positions of intercourse leered from the corners, from behind the king size round bed; also on the ceiling they seemed intimately wound around each other.

They hypnotized the detective, his head swivelling around, his body shaking from cold chills of shock, his manhood regions on fire as if the men reached out to stroke him. One model, whom he recognized, seemed to be staring invitingly at him and he could almost hear his words.

Surrounded by the almost pulsing photos, memories of

similar encounters flooded back. He had to escape. Struggling with his reaction, his heartbeat escalated until it pounded and throbbed in every limb. The impact of the photos, as irresistible as the Lorelei's enchanted songs on the Rhine River, threatened to overpower his weak flesh. Shamed and nauseated he turned and fled.

He seemed to be poised at the edge of a cliff that over-shadowed a bottomless pit. He needed to withdraw quickly into the safety of his new life, where clean-minded people brought true fulfilment and not shame.

He was leaning against the wall by the elevator, pressing the down button with perspiring palms, when Bradley caught up with him. "Tony, we'll finish up here. It's a test and you've made the right decision. Call Pastor Bob. We'll work on this business until you get back to your office."

Breathing with more control, he argued, "Do I need to phone Pastor Bob? It was just the suddenness of seeing those sexually explicit photos that derailed me—or was it? I don't want to fight old temptations again. I'm free of them."

"Phone Pastor Bob. He'll rescue you from this minefield."

Tony nodded then rode the elevator to the ground floor where the commissionaire opened the glass front door for him. As he took deep breaths of cool air, the normal surroundings of sunlight, lampposts, traffic, grass boulevard removed the threat he experi-enced in the graphic photos. Although the attack passed, the intensity of his reaction shocked him. He had thought himself to be worldly-wise and fully in control of his emotions.

Perhaps it was the unexpectedness of the encounter, or the concealing darkness around the photos or the fact his body had reacted in the old way, but for a feverish moment the old feelings had reappeared. However, by relegating them to the past, he had succeeded in passing his first test in his walk with Jesus.

Hoping the busy minister would answer his phone, he dialled the church number.

An hour later, Tony parked his Mustang near the church side door, leapt out, and entered Pastor Bob's office waiting room.

The secretary looked up startled and alert. After giving him a cursory glance to check whether he currently took drugs or alcohol, she asked, "Do you have an appointment, Mr ...?"

"Mr Moretti. Tony Moretti. Yes, I phoned earlier this morning, Miss ..." He raised his eyebrows to learn her name. In the vernacular she was a dish. To his surprise, he found her attractive. Black hair curled under in an attractive pageboy around a creamy, flawless complexion and rosy cheeks. He expected her eyes to be liquid violets; instead they reminded him of warm comforting chocolate.

She turned her eyes away, responding distantly, "I'm Mrs Oakes. You do have an appointment. As soon as the pastor finishes talking on the phone, he will be with you."

Taking his card she walked gracefully to place it on the pastor's desk.

Tony, stunned but pleased that he could admire a woman, whistled softly.

31

Mrs Oakes resumed her typing, carefully inserting letters into matching envelopes. Other pages she carried to the photocopier, feeding the machine, and dislodging wisps of wavy hair from her neat pageboy. Intrigued by this woman who never once looked at him, Tony riffled half-heartedly through a magazine.

Presently the pastor emerged, apologized for the wait and ushered him into his roomy office. From the easy chair opposite the pastor, Tony studied his mentor. He noted Pastor Bob was of average height, but nevertheless his appearance was striking because of the intelligence in his face. He had thick, dark hair, slightly sprinkled with grey, deep set black eyes and a long, straight nose. Even when he relaxed, there was an energy within him. Putting his fingertips together, he expectantly waited for Tony to enlighten him regarding his surprise visit.

"Pastor, I've been set free—gloriously free. All attraction for males has left me. However, this morning we searched an apartment where pornography involving males in sexual activities lined the walls. Those pictures alarmed and disturbed—the pull on my subconscious was overpowering. I had to get away from them.

"Because I've committed to being a Christian, I refuse to return to that bondage. Temptations lurk in hidden corners, but I can't run from them when it involves my work. How can I protect myself from realistic images that try to bring on the old fantasies?"

"Tony, you quote scriptures even under your breath, for God's power is in His Word. Revelation 12:11: *'They overcame him by the blood of the Lamb and by the word of their testimony; ...'* The blood of the lamb is Jesus' blood spilt on Calvary that gives us not only salvation but protection, health, wholeness—the whole package. You say to yourself 'I cover myself, my spirit, body, mind with the blood of Jesus', and Satan can't touch you. As well think or say powerful scriptures such as: 'Greater is He who is in me than he who is in the world.' In our Bible studies we'll teach more about this to provide the faith to back it up. For what we put in our heart—what we believe—we possess by speaking it from our mouth. Very simple—totally effective. Are you reading your Bible every day?"

"Yes, I am. I'm also buying resource books that enable me to understand it better. It is simply written but the nuggets have to be dug for. I'm quoting Proverbs. Before I head to my office and if I'm not out of line, your secretary, Mrs Oakes—please tell me about her."

A deep furrow appeared between Pastor Bob's eyes. "Rita Oakes has been a widow since her husband died of a brain tumour ten months ago The year before, when he learned he had a tumour, they attended church hoping for and then believing for a miracle. They accepted Christ and they thought he was healed. Possibly he was—God responds to faith. But they returned to their former living patterns and thoughts, roaring around on his motorcycle instead of spending time to build his faith. Consequently, the tumour returned. In a short time he was dead."

"I'm sorry. Did she lose her faith?"

"Like you this morning when you were tested, she set her face like flint to God. Willie was alright because through it all he knew Jesus. It wasn't perfect, but it was alright."

"I wondered. I detected a loneliness about her. Maybe wishful thinking."

"Oh the loneliness is there right enough, but in her eyes she is still married—she clings to her identity of being Willie's widow. She grieves, for they were very much in love."

"Pastor, it's becoming clearer to me that the way we see ourselves, our self-identity, makes or breaks us."

"Yes. It is important to recognize ourselves as Jesus' brother or sister, God's covenant children."

"The loss of my lover is recent also. It didn't even end in a way that we could be friends. Yet, I'm encouraged in my new life because I found a woman attractive."

Pastor Bob laughed, "Tread lightly with Rita. Give her time and space."

"Of course. I'm only wanting to make new friends, Christian ones, who will help me to mature in the Christian life."

"Nice to see you, Tony. Come any time. I'm delighted with your commitment and I'm sure the Lord is, too."

"Each day grows more astonishing. Thank you Pastor."

On his way out, Tony smiled at the hardworking secretary, bringing a blush to her cheek. Then Pastor Bob flew out of his office, "Tony, you like to be here most days, don't you?"

"Yes," Tony rested his hand on the doorknob.

"Have you considered joining the choir? They rehearse on Thursday nights. You belong to it, Rita. Do they need new members?"

The chocolate eyes developed dark pools, "Yes we do. The choir can always use a male voice. Do you sing tenor or bass?"

The sudden proposal rocked Tony slightly, "My voice is a shade above a bullfrog's croak; I must be a bass."

"You'll do," beamed the pastor; then confronted by two pairs of puzzled eyes frowning at him, he retreated to his office.

Over a coffee at the Station, Tony shared with Bradley, "I've been approached about joining the church choir and I think I will."

Bradley choked on his swallow of coffee, "Have they heard you sing?"

"No. Maybe I could whistle while everyone else sings. Maybe I could mouth the words."

Bradley stroked his chin, thoughtfully assessing the gleam in Tony's eyes. "Is there some motivation for this new activity that you're not telling me?"

133

Tony grinned at his curious partner. "Maybe. Maybe I'm just an undiscovered Bruce Springsteen. Whatever—I'll not be working late on Thursday evenings."

The next Thursday, freshly showered, wearing casual slacks with a knife-like press, and a blue sweater, Tony reported to Len Jefferson, the choir director. Before he could detail his lack of musical ability, the big baritone-chested man shook his hand and instructed him, "Stand at the end of the top row with the men. You'll overlook three rows of women. If you don't know the tune, sing *a sotto.* Or just move your lips and look happy. Welcome."

Tony tucked that advice away to ruminate on later and looked up at his three male choristers: one was chest high on Tony with long hair falling like a waterfall from his pointed face; the next came to Tony's chin, was balding and weighed at least 200 pounds; the third one's head skimmed Tony's eyebrows, had a muscular, well proportioned body.

While they greeted him with handshakes, the shortest one, who looked as if he could slip through a keyhole, at first looked alarmed then threw back his head and guffawed. "Sergeant, we meet again. You put me away for three years."

Tony knew the young man looked familiar, yet not the same as he had when they caught him. "John Avery. Are the three years up already? You weren't easy to catch."

"I was released early for good behaviour. I want to thank you. I found Jesus behind those prison bars. My life changed for the better because I have a good job that I enjoy, and I live for Jesus."

"Congratulations. I didn't recognize you. I'm a brand new convert. It really makes me want to sing when I hear your good news. Are any other prison alumni in this church?"

John shook his head.

Len Jefferson clapped loudly—the signal to arrange themselves on the steps. Fortunately some of the women were tall so Tony did not tower over everyone. Not so fortunately, Rita Oakes sang at the end of the bottom row.

32

On a mellow October Sunday morning that hinted of frosty nights to come and as the harvest moon waned, Janet reached for the jangling phone. Her two offspring were too sleepy from watching a late night movie to pick it up first.

"Good morning," she chirped, dropping a piece of egg on her housecoat. "It's not that early. I can take a surprise. Oh yes. How marvellous! The kids will want to come. Where is the church? We'll find it. A lovely surprise. Thank you."

"Dale, Luci, get your bods down here. We're going to the Hickory Hills Christian Fellowship at the corner of Main and Hillside Streets. Mandy and her family will be there, too."

Dale surfaced first, muttering, "What's going on? That's supposed to be an alive church. I won't be able to sleep through the sermon."

"Don't be silly. You'll be wide awake. Where is Luci?" Janet scooped crisp bacon strips and lightly turned eggs onto a plate for Dale, who grabbed his own toast from the toaster.

"I'm here," Luci yawned as she held the door for Toby to enter. "Oh good, Toby loves bacon."

Sighing pointedly Janet threw more bacon into the pan. "I can't tell you the reason we're going there; it's a surprise." She grinned impishly, knowing aroused curiosity in her teenagers drove them to distraction. "It's a celebration." She broke into singing "Gloria in Excelsis."

Toby howled. Luci groaned. Dale looked stoic.

"You celebrate over every little thing," Luci complained.

"When something good happens, we best celebrate at once. The downers come often enough. And we are commanded to rejoice. Eat your breakfast; we leave in three-quarters of an hour." She took the front stairs two at a time.

The teenagers, already curious, caught Janet's joy and complied. Within the hour, Janet proudly ushered her handsome son and pretty daughter through the doors of Hickory Hills Fellowship. Mandy, who was watching for them, stood up and waved them into the pew in front of her family. They greeted their friends before sitting down to read the bulletins clutched in their hands. Dale spotted it first. Luci was too busy checking out the young people floating in the aisles.

"I know why we're here."

"Oh don't be mean. Tell me."

Dale pointed to a name in the list of people to be water baptised that morning.

"Oh Mommy! (in her excitement Luci reverted to her childish term) Tony is to be baptised and we'll see him dipped." She gave her brother a high five. Mandy laughed and signalled the same to Janet. As well, she gave her friend an encouraging squeeze, for she knew in spite of Janet's joy, despair lurked because Ryan was not a participant, too.

When the choir entered, Tony spotted the group immediately. Surprised and delighted he forgot to sing until his short pal jabbed his ribs. He smiled like a contestant for a toothpaste commercial and mouthed 'thank you' to Janet. In response she gave the V sign and he knew that his sins were truly forgiven.

During the offertory the young woman beside Rita in the choir's front row whispered, "Did you see the warm looks exchanged between the lady with the two children and the hunk above us? Maybe she's his girlfriend."

"Maybe. I hope so—I'm not into that scene. Sing. That's

136

why you're here."

The friend, unperturbed by Rita's sharpness, sang and was secretly pleased that Rita's reaction denoted perhaps a feeble interest in Tony. Rita chastised herself, for she had no right to be curious about Tony's personal life. That was his business—not hers. He could have three wives for all she cared.

Later in the service Pastor Bob stepped forward to speak God's truths directly into His people's hearts. Snippets of the sermon even registered with Dale.

"In the act of baptism we identify with Jesus' death on the Cross. Therefore God promises that like His resurrection we too are raised up as new creations. Before, we were dead due to the world's traps of sin. Now the Christian comes alive with the new life of Christ. That is why we shout, "Hallelujah!" at the victory of the Cross.

"You have witnessed these people's death and resurrection."

At the coffee hour Dale saw Anna with her parents. When she smiled at him, his heart pounded, his spirit soared and he went to her like steel to a magnet. Her parents greeted him warmly, enquiring about his connection to Tony. He explained Tony was a friend of his parents. Satisfied, they turned to speak to their companions while Dale and Anna raided the cookie table.

The rest of Janet's entourage surrounded a radiant Tony who hugged Mandy and Janet to show his gratitude for their prayers. Members of the congregation welcomed him into God's kingdom and their church, allowing the two women to drink their tea peacefully. When they had emptied their cups, Rita appeared with a teapot to refill them. She hesitated, wanting to say their presence gave the baptisms a meaningful blessing. But noticing Janet's sad eyes, she introduced herself and moved on.

Mandy studied the pain that surfaced briefly on Janet's face. Taking her arm she guided their steps to a quiet area where she lanced Janet's wound with a direct question: "Are you worried about Ryan? He is master of his own destiny—not you."

"I know, but his destiny affects mine and that of the children. They are confused, for they think his nightmare is like a fierce storm flying across the sky and it will blow away. And parts of the Bible are no comfort. Last night Dale discovered in Leviticus that stark verse: 'If a man lies with a man as one lies with a woman, both of them have done what is detestable. They must be put to death; their blood will be on their own heads.' (Leviticus 20; 13)

"What could I tell Dale? Sin brings death—sometimes physically but always spiritually. We both realised Ryan is in trouble big time, especially for abandoning God. However, Dale knows God never abandons His people and has made a way out by Jesus dying on that horrible cross. Mandy, help me to believe."

Mandy remembered an incident involving another friend: "A friend of mine was in Germany and visited an art gallery in Munich, which houses a vast collection of masterpieces—mostly biblical. When she came to Rembrandt's painting of the Crucifixion, she noticed that he had painted himself in it kneeling at the foot of the Cross. Suddenly she knew that she too was kneeling there. When she returned to her hotel God assured my friend that her dead husband was fine and everything was going to be alright.

"In our weakness all of us need to kneel at the foot of the Cross to receive forgiveness and have His life-changing love flow over us and into us. Our prayers helped Tony catch God's vision and accept Jesus' love—surely God will hear our cries for Ryan."

Mandy put down her cup to hug Janet, saying: "We know that is God's will, but He's given us free will. Ryan has to decide that is what he wants."

"Some members of the church at Corinth chose a bad lifestyle." Pastor Bob's strong authoritative voice coming from behind the women made them jump. "But the apostle Paul makes this amazing statement: 'Some of you were once like that. But you were cleansed, you were made holy; you were made right with God by calling on the name of the Lord Jesus Christ and by the Spirit of our God'."

"Oh, I like that verse better than Leviticus. Where is it in the

Bible? It restores my hope."

Pastor Bob hugged Janet. "It's 1 Corinthians 6: 11. God does not have favourites. He loves Ryan as much as He does Tony and us." Then he moved on to speak to others.

Janet gave Mandy a wan smile. She determined not to be depressed. She would not succumb. She wouldn't. God told **her** to rejoice in everything—to give thanks. But more than ever she wanted to see Ryan transformed by the Holy Spirit into a person who lived in harmony with God, experiencing His love and peace. She and God would be holding many talks about Ryan's salvation.

33

November 1985

Anna groaned. The yellow ribbon she needed was submerged under piles of ribbons, buttons, doilies, scraps of cloth, wrapping paper on the dining-room table. "What a mess!" she sighed. "But I'm still hopeful I can find some attractive bits that will decorate my shoe box for the Box Social."

When their Youth Pastor in desperation decreed they would sponsor one to meet their money-raising goal, he answered all doubts with the statement, "Trust me in this. You'll enjoy it."

Anna greeted a matronly woman with swinging auburn hair who stuck her head in the room and who shook her head in amazement.

"Mother, how can I decorate my box for our Box Social? I do want it to be a work of art that Dale will know is mine. I'd never heard of a box social until Pastor Bob came up with the idea because November is a lousy month to raise money by washing cars. We're only half way to raising the money for our mission trip next winter break."

"It's an old-fashioned idea but a good one for romances. Your great-grandmother met your great-grandfather when he bid on her box. At barn dances in rural areas the girls packed lunches for young men to bid on. Even after World War II they held them. A good auctioneer ensured every box was auctioned off to unsuspecting local beaus who blindly bid on one. But they were wary because they had to eat the contents with the girl who brought the box, making every bid a game of chance. Shy lads rolled their eyes when they were prodded into bidding and hoped the ground would open up so they could disappear. But it was great fun—often starting a few romances." She eyed her daughter speculatively.

"I think it's more nerve-racking on the girls than the boys," she continued, "the males choose the box lunch. You can only watch and hope the boy you like bids on yours."

"It's awkward. If Brent guesses which box is mine and buys it, then I must spend the evening with him and ignore Dale. What if he bids on gorgeous Susan's lunch? Everything she does is upscale—she'll probably pack caviar in her box. I'd be ready to pull her hair if she sat close to Dale. Anyway, I must decorate this box and pack the lunch in it before the movie and auction tonight."

"Choose a theme relevant to Dale's interests. Also, use the loaf of homemade bread for roast beef sandwiches. Dill pickles will go well. And I remember Grandmother said every box held a butter tart or a sandcherry tart piled high with whipped cream and a date square."

"Mom, I'll follow your suggestions. Later, I'll tie a yellow ribbon around the box."

She jumped as the backdoor slammed, announcing the return of Tom, her ten-year-old brother. "Here comes the monster. Have you any lizards or snakes in your pockets?"

"Nope, none of those," he answered innocently with a noncommittal shrug. "They're all hibernating."

"Good thing." The women briefly wondered if they should search his pockets, but since cold November weather drove creepy crawlies into snug winter homes, they didn't bother. With another shrug and avoiding eye contact, Tom headed for the cookie jar.

By six o'clock, Anna was finishing her box with a wide yellow ribbon tied at one end in a massive bow. The box's sides rippled with blue bric-à-brac like a river in which yellow candies swam fish-like. On the top a galaxy of small colourful flowers built up to a peak under the bow.

"It is elaborate, isn't it?" She looked to her mother for approval.

"Dear, it's just great. You designed carefully and Dale will love it."

From under the table, Tom piped up, "Don't eat everything in the box."

Anna peered under the table, "Why not?"

However, the doorbell ringing stopped Anna from pursuing the reason for his statement. After hiding the box in a bag, she hurried to open the door for Dale. He greeted her smiling mother, held Anna's coat for her and offered to carry the bag.

"As long as you don't peek at the box," she grinned.

"Of course not; but I can test its weight."

"Bye Mom." Anna walked to the car humming: "And around her neck she wore a yellow ribbon ..." but stopped when they arrived at the church. She thought, 'Surely he'll get the clue. I hope no one else tied as dominant a yellow ribbon as I did. This is agony.'

At the church the girls deposited their boxes in the kitchen near the auditorium to be set out on a long table during the intermission of the movie, *Quo Vadis.* Prior to the burning of Rome, the youth leader called for lights and for the auction to begin. The boys circled the table examining the boxes. Anna had half sung, half hummed the 'Yellow Ribbon' so long that the words registered in Dale's mind. 'Aha,' he thought, 'a yellow ribbon. I'll look for a box with a yellow ribbon.' It wasn't hard to do, for three boxes matched the description. 'I'll bet Anna didn't bargain on that. How do I decide which one is hers?' His hands began to feel clammy. 'If I don't bid on hers, this party will be a disaster. Maybe I should bid on all three—no, no. That wouldn't help.'

Beside him, Paul bent over boxes as though half blind to inspect their design. At one he breathed deeply saying, "Mmmmm." Then he checked out his friend, "Aren't you getting dizzy from circling so much?"

"Shut up. I'm concentrating." All three box tops bloomed with pretty flowers, so he checked their sides. The first was wrapped in gold; the second had dogs chasing each other around it; then he clued into the third, which had water in which yellow fish played.

"That's for my canoeing. Yes. Clever girl. I've found her box. Paul, why do you bow to every box?"

"I was smelling them, my dear Watson. My nose ferrets out the most delectable delicacies."

"Oh, which one?"

"Forget it. I'm not telling you—it's mine." He smiled smugly.

With the girls arrayed on the west wall, the boys stood in the middle to place their bids. Dale whispered to Paul, "How much money do you have?"

"I've a twenty. And you?"

"The same. There's a cap of twenty dollars on the bidding. Thank goodness."

The auctioneer, a well built man wearing a ten gallon hat, strode importantly through the doors. Holding up a box chosen at random he called for opening bids. After five minutes of his describing the box in glowing adjectives, a brave boy bid on it. He was rewarded by winning it for $5.00.

Nervous, giggling girls parted like ground opening in an earthquake and then again formed a united front to allow the box's creator to present the lunch to the boy. He visibly grinned with relief that his performance was over. Together they walked to an eating table to sit and enjoy their friends' suspense.

Uncertainty swayed the other girls. In their keyed-up agitation, they emitted squeals of excitement as each person called out a bid. Some couldn't watch when their box came up for auction. At the words, "Sold to this handsome fellow", they dared to peek at their evening partner. But a few faces fell when they realised the wrong person had bought their box.

Paul bid on a box decorated with an icing sugar design that went for ten dollars. From the mob of girls, Jane, a skinny sixteen year old with a ponytail and a happy face brought the box to him, then they settled into seats in the back row. Dale heard her saying, "My mom's the best cook. You'll enjoy the lunch."

After what seemed an eternity, Anna's box was lifted in the auctioneer's hands. Before Dale opened his mouth, a voice behind him shouted, "$2.00".

Not to be outbid by Brent, Dale yelled, "$4.00."

"$10.00," said Brent, making Dale ballistic, with: "$14.00."

"Whoa," the auctioneer tipped back his ten gallon hat as he pounded his gavel. Dale's heart skipped a beat, for he thought that ended the bidding and he had lost.

"You may bid $2.00 up or under $2.00 but not more than $2.00. Now we'll go on from the $4.00 bid."

Brent said, "$6.00," giving Dale an intimidating glare.

Anna stopped breathing, unable to watch.

After $16.00, a strange voice yelled, "$17.00."

Dale groaned, "Now what do I do?"

Brent without thinking yelled, "19.00," enabling Dale to close the bidding at $20.00. The stranger melted into the crowd before Dale could glimpse him.

"Going, going, gone to this lucky young man," the auctioneer pounded his gavel and pointed to Dale.

Dale, sagging at his knees, quickly paid for the box. After a relieved Anna presented it to him, they pulled up chairs beside Paul and his new friend.

Paul asked, "Anna, what's in that box? I saw it move."

"Don't be daft," Dale answered, untying the yellow bow.

"Hi Jane," Anna said. "Let me dish out the food, Dale."

Lifting the lid, she screamed. A pink nose and whiskers twitched beside the wax paper-wrapped sandwiches. The box landed on Dale, who pushed it on Paul, so he could calm Anna. The mouse ran down Paul's leg. Jane, who was scared to death of mice, leapt onto the table top, shrieking as if Armageddon had arrived.

Paul with the speed of light removed his shoe, keeping it poised in his hand as he chased the equally terrified mouse. He

144

whammed it with so strong a blow that blood squirted for a metre.

The blood sent a number of nauseated girls holding their mouths into the washroom, where Anna was trying to calm Jane. When the poor mouse had been removed, Paul and Dale doubled up with laughter.

"We better stop this, Paul. The girls aren't amused."

"Right. But I think I deserve a bite of lunch for delivering that mortal blow." Paul extracted a hefty sandwich on which he happily munched between chuckles. Dale's hunger pangs needed assuaging, too, so he also found a sandwich to devour.

The girls peeked out of the ladies room.

"Those cads are eating without us." Anna grabbed Jane and they descended on the unperturbed boys. "What are you doing, eating without us!" they chorused.

"Hey. We waited so long we thought you weren't hungry." Dale, shifting his eyes guiltily, tried to appease them.

"Humph!!" The girls, who couldn't maintain their anger, laughed until all four were weak and holding their sides.

Paul said, "Jane, your lunch is so delicious I'd go through it all again."

She beamed proudly, "When we lived in the country, Mom won most of the cooking prizes at the county fair."

"We're going to purr along just fine. Your mom's cooking is heavenly."

In Dale's box the mouse had eaten a few mouthfuls of tart leaving the sandwiches for Anna and Dale. In between bites Anna invited suggestions for suitable punishment for Tom. She apologized for the surprise, hoping Dale was not disappointed with his twenty dollar lunch.

Putting down his sandwich, he took Anna's hand and gently stroked it. In his eyes she found the answer she sought. When she smiled with eyes for him alone, he silently thanked the little critter, instinctively knowing her support would buoy him up if storm clouds gathered.

34

March 1986

The day was bitterly cold with a raw March wind blowing that heralded an approaching storm. Ryan shivered uncontrollably, and told himself it was not because he was afraid to die. In his family, the men lived into their nineties, so his life span was predetermined to be long. Still, a persistent doubt nagged his mind; maybe he was the exception. His fever should have left days ago.

The ringing of his phone jarred his nerves.

"I'm sorry to phone you so early in the morning, Mr Telfer," Dr Reid's nurse said quietly. The rest of her words jumbled in Ryan's mind, making her message incoherent. He shook his head to clear it, hoping when she repeated her message, it would sound more positive. It didn't.

Why was she phoning him? Ahh! Two days ago he visited Dr Reid for a checkup and medicine for the chest rattle that had settled in like a cowbird's chick in a sparrow's nest, depleting his body's vigour.

As efficient as a recorded phone message, the nurse intoned, "Dr Reid is extremely concerned about your test results. He expects you in his office at 2 p.m. this afternoon. If you have someone close to you, bring him with you."

"Alright. Alright. I'll be there." The evening before the checkup, a slim long-haired young actor came home with him from the gay club. After their 'deed of darkness' as the youth described it, he told Ryan he looked somewhat like a friend who

146

developed symptoms of the virus that led to AIDS.

"Better see your doctor. It's a killer. Ta." Picking up crisp bills placed on the dresser for him, he left. Ryan glowered sullenly at his retreating back, wondering how he found himself in such an unbearably lonely state.

After Tony moved out, Ryan prowled the gay bars looking for a new companion. It was a dragged out routine—sitting in a key spot to survey others in the crowded peak times—watching eyes light up at the entrance of a new young man. Sometimes the youth conversed with Ryan. More often the prospect moved on looking for a more suitable stranger with whom to go home for the night. Ryan often walked to his car alone.

But in that scene he found Abner, a gay pornographer who brought into his studio young struggling actors with physiques like Greek gods. After he hired them as models for his pornographic photos and videos, he operated a sideline. Abner also hustled introductions for visits to 'johns' between three and four a.m. Scornful of Ryan's middle-aged physique, he called him only when more important 'johns' were unavailable, to tell that he had a "stunning beauty" in town for a shoot and could he scrape together thirty dollars. When Abner hadn't phoned for a while, Ryan chanced the gay bars. Still more and more he resorted to his fantasies. Waiting for visits from money-strapped athletic California actors provoked anxiety.

Even the next day after his last nocturnal visitor, his ill health enveloped him like a depressing cloud. In the physician's office, Dr Reid had sympathized and hoped that the prescription for penicillin and bed rest would rid him of the pneumonia in his chest. The rattling sound when he coughed had lessened but not disappeared. The doctor promised to contact Ryan immediately as soon as his tests' results for the immune system came back.

The report was in the doctor's office. Still gripping the phone as if it were the source of his pain, he wondered why the doctor wanted someone with him that afternoon. Who should he call? He had many acquaintances who laughed at his dirty jokes, but this wasn't funny. They wouldn't come. There was only one

147

person—Gramps.

Resolutely dialling the farm number, he waited. His father's arthritis slowed his walk to the phone.

"Yup. Old man Telfer here."

"Young man Telfer here. How are you Dad?"

"Glad to hear your voice. How are you on this east wind of a day?"

"Not the best. I had a checkup last week with Dr Reid. He has results but wants me to bring someone with me this afternoon when he talks to me. Are you interested in coming?"

Ryan heard his father's sharp intake of breath. "Of course. My old Ford truck will be parked in front of your place at one o'clock. It will be better than hearing your news secondhand."

Although he restored the phone to its normal position, Ryan could not restore his pre-call normal feeling. He roamed the duplex apartment, mentally conjuring up deadly diseases that might be the cause of the doctor's urgency. He clenched his fists and shuddered. If he was going to be sick, why hadn't it happened after his abuse as a child, and saved all these years of misery and fear. No. Maybe it was just Doc's way of hospitalizing him for pneumonia, he comforted himself.

Holding that thought he listened to his messages on the answering device. It held four messages. The first three regarding potential buyers he disregarded, but the last one, Dale, he played twice. "Dad, I would like to take Anna to a movie Saturday night. Could I postpone my visit to the following Saturday? If I don't hear from you I'll assume it's okay. If you need me for anything before then, just phone. Hope your fever is gone."

He smiled. Dale seemed to like Anna a lot. He wished them well. Although he cherished Dale and his loyalty, they had never communicated in depth. He guessed at Dale's degree of interest in Anna. He wondered about his son's plans for his life. Whatever they were, he didn't want to hinder them.

Ryan slipped into his easy chair, and dozed until a knock at the door announced his father's arrival. Gramps steered his way

148

past a pile of books, around a few boxes that had held groceries, until he found a chair unoccupied by carelessly tossed articles. However, Gramps saw only Ryan's white drawn face.

"Dad. Good you're here." Ryan did not pursue a line of chatter.

Gramps held his questions, for his son looked as if a 20 ton truck had run him down. "Let's get this over with. I'll drive."

Ryan nodded, picking up his jacket. "Dr Reid's office is on Queen Street."

His head ached with each jolt of the old truck, causing his eyes to water. Gramps didn't look at him; just at the traffic ahead until he pulled what he lovingly called his "heap of junk" into the clinic's parking lot. Gramps' stomach rolled with the same queasiness he experienced when Wifey was diagnosed with cancer. Ryan felt he rode a runaway locomotive that was gaining momentum.

Inside the clinic the nurse took a quick look at Ryan, then ushered him in as the next patient to where the doctor stood holding his folder. While his compassion was evident in his gentle manner, his helplessness covered his face.

"Ryan, your tests revealed what we feared—you have the antibodies of the disease that we hoped would stay in Africa, but which is now here among the gay population."

Gramps interrupted. "What is this disease? Why is it feared?"

"It's only in the last year they have developed a blood test for AIDS. Only recently has it been identified with a name— Acquired Immune Deficiency Syndrome. It's the final stages of HIV or Human Immunodeficiency Virus. Six months ago Ryan contracted HIV which can last a few years before developing AIDS. Unfortunately, Ryan's is a fast-moving form."

Ryan opened his mouth to speak, then gulped air and closed it again. An involuntary shudder vibrated in his diaphragm. A blow on the head could not have stunned him more.

With a muttered oath, his frustrated father implored, "You must have a medicine—some cure—for this unheard-of illness.

149

Help us, for God's sake."

"We have checked all the drug companies," Dr Reid continued. "There is no drug for this horrible disease. It is so new to us that we hardly know where to start to look for something—anything—that would cure it or even slow its development."

Gramps stared at him, his skin drained of colour. "I'm sure...," he said between dry lips, "I'm sure there must be something you can do."

Dr Reid spoke with intense feeling. "I can only prescribe for the various disease symptoms. There is no cure. Ryan, I feel I should tell you that you have at least three months, hopefully more, before it takes you."

"Thank you," Ryan whispered. And he stood unsteadily, ashen-faced and old looking, leaning on his father to find his way out.

35

The next few mornings were the worst in Ryan's life. On day three, he lay on his back staring up at the ceiling. The duplex was silent. It was shortly after six, an hour before his usual wake-up time. He could think of nothing to get up for and his mind rampaged in circles. He was dying and only his dad cared. Alone and in despair, he couldn't bear to consider the darkness ahead. Even though he knew he had to plan out his final few months of life, he had no idea where or how to begin.

Robert had warned that with the advent of the 1980s, the loathsome disease, AIDS—no longer confined to Africa—had infiltrated the North American scene. Like the plague of the Middle Ages, no one knew its source nor means of escaping its murderous onslaught. Three of Robert's partners died of AIDS, leaving him tormented lest he, too, join the epidemic numbers succumbing to the disease. Not realising that it was transmitted through intercourse, Ryan unconcernedly slept with Robert that night.

Finally, he thought it was stupid lying there thinking about it. He got up, washed, dressed, made a cup of coffee, then headed to the library. While the reference librarian showing him the AIDS books treated him civilly, she not only glanced at him with a peculiar expression but also kept a safe distance between them as they walked between the bookshelves.

In the publications he read that AIDS not only reduced healthy people to breeding fields for viruses; lack of scientific research and public information brought fear, misunderstanding and discrimination. It was a modern-day leprosy that was attributed mainly to gays. A pal at the gay club who was suspected of having the disease, tried to have a haircut. The barber refused to cut his hair, shunning him openly. In vain the AIDS victim tried to reassure him that in 1984 they found it was not transmitted by casual contact but in liquids through sexual intercourse, infected blood and drug injection needles. Further protestations were useless, for the barber's prejudice was too strong—he simply shut out the truth.

Dr Reid told Ryan he knew people who refused to go to a church or club that accepted people with AIDS. Unfortunately, many people transferred their fear of AIDS to people who they suspected might have the disease. Further proof came from another sleeping partner whose job was terminated on the pretext that the firm needed to regroup and cut back. That had not happened until he showed AIDS symptoms in his body.

To clarify his emotions Ryan drew a cartoon in which a group of people under a cloud of irrational fears stood with arms stiff and hands upright to push away a group of infected gays. In between he saw his children whose arms reached out to him in love and who were also being shunned by the fearful people.

While he still had some body strength, he determined to remove himself from their lives. His children would not suffer for his mistakes. Although his life was ending, their adulthood lay ahead of them. And he longed for them to have a good start—a normal life. Therefore he would cut all contact by disappearing into the city's maelstrom where not even detective Tony could unearth him.

Where could he live that they couldn't find him? He wanted to be near Dr Reid, whose friendship and compassion gave him an element of peace. Ironically Dr Reid's only rant was his inability to provide a cure.

Ryan reflected on how, in healthier days, Janet and he talked about child support which could be erratic because he had to sell houses to have an income. She had assured him her teacher's salary covered all essential expenses, so he had sent money whenever a house sold. In a way, having to live as though the support money might not come on the third of the month had prepared them for this time when none would be sent. But then the children worked to help the cash flow. Thinking of Luci's hard- earned cash from dog walking, he almost smiled. In spite of being an inadequate landlord, rent from the duplex would hopefully cover his own expenses. Furthermore, by simplifying his lifestyle, he accepted the strictures of AIDS—he was an outcast.

*   *   *   *   *

Rain beat relentlessly as he steered his car towards the city's outskirts. Cruising the motel strip he stopped at one that appeared large enough to have a suite he could rent by the month. The few suites they had were too large for one person. Two motels further he found his new home. The large livingroom contained a dining table, sofa, two chairs, a TV. At the back a kitchen provided facilities for preparing meals. On one side an open stairway led to a loft where he could put his own bed. He liked the fact it was sparsely furnished, so that a few of his own furniture pieces would fill spaces.

"I'll take it. Can I park my car at the rear?"

"I don't see why not. You can get to it through the door in the kitchen."

"Good. I'll move in tomorrow."

The rain stopped the next day as Ryan used Gramps' truck to move his belongings into his new abode. When he returned the vehicle, Gramps propelled his son into the farmhouse to eat the supper he had prepared.

Gramps' heart expanded and broke simultaneously, for he knew that his formerly robust son suffered constantly from his illness. As a father he noted in Ryan's eyes, his leanness, and in his debilitating sweats that AIDS already played havoc with his body.

"Son, you lived in this house with your mother and me from the moment we brought you home from the hospital until you married in your twenties. This is your home—whatever I have is yours. Come back and live here with me."

153

Having finished half the spicy stew Gramps had put in front of him, Ryan set it aside and grasped his father's hand. "Thanks, Dad, but I can't. Your pain would hurt more than the sickness will. I'll probably be on pain killers for my torment, but you won't be. I'll cope."

On the borderline of tears, Gramps simply shrugged, "The offer stands if you change your mind. You will phone me every week."

"Yes. I owe you that. I won't give you my phone number because I don't want anyone in contact with me. Please try to explain to Janet and the kids why I feel this way is the only option. They'll have to accept it."

"Of course. It's a bitter pill for those teenagers to swallow. However, they're young and still adaptable—I hope."

The two men faced each other. How did one say a final goodbye to one's father?

With a wave and an "Au revoir," Ryan pulled his car out of the farmyard past squawking hens onto the county road. Gramps, as usual when distressed, opened the barn door, skirting strewn straw to talk to his attentive cows

*   *   *   *   *

The next day, Janet rejoiced as Frank, with whom she had worked strenuously to help him understand a math problem, arrived at the correct answer. She felt as though the 'aha' experience were hers, too. Still, she was relieved at 3:30 p.m. to shut her classroom door and stride to her car. Because Gramps was coming for supper, she planned a gourmet feast that would plant a few pounds on him.

Within fifteen minutes she donned her favourite apron adorned with blue cows. While she was brewing and stirring, Dale galloped downstairs two steps at a time.

"Mom, I tried to phone Dad, but a Bell recording announced, 'This number is no longer in service.' Do you think he hasn't paid his phone bill or perhaps he's moved? If so, why didn't he warn us?"

Janet put down her wooden stirring spoon. "I don't know,

Dale. Gramps should be here soon. On the phone he sounded so sad and tense. Whatever is going on, it's probably why he invited himself to come tonight. If you see Luci, tell her to be prompt for dinner."

"I'll tell her we're having dog for dinner," Dale muttered, ignoring Janet's look of stoic exasperation.

Gramps' truck rattled into the parking spot beside Janet's car. Nostalgically he pictured Ryan carrying two young children to greet him. In those days they waited impatiently for his arrival and scrambled out at the first squeal of the truck's brakes. He longed for a time machine that would carry them all back to the good times.

He wished he didn't have to share his bad news. Maybe it wouldn't press down on him like a locked trapdoor when all family members knew. Their reaction could be volcanic.

Inside the kitchen he smelled barbecued ribs, tender squash, and succulent roasted potatoes, and his insides reacted with an urgent hunger. Janet hugged him, telling Dale to hang his coat. Luci threw herself on him for her bear hug.

The meal seemed to take hours. Forbidden to question Gramps until he finished his meal, Dale and Luci ate staring into their plates. Gramps tried to engage them in conversation about school, their teachers or some recent memory when their grandmother lived. But they merely waited to hear news of their father.

They served themselves small pieces of apple pie made from Grandmother's famous recipe and waited while Gramps nervously ate his portion. Finally, Janet lit two lamps in the family room.

Gramps eyed the children in silence—Dale's partially understanding face and Luci's fearful attitude.

"Children," Gramps said forcing his words, "I have unpleasant news about your father. Dale is right. He has moved. To protect himself and even more to protect you, his whereabouts are unknown. He has promised to phone me every

155

week." He paused, but Dale urged him on. "Why? We're on his side."

Gramps looked at Janet, who nodded: "It's better they know the facts rather than have their imaginations run amok."

"Six months ago your father was diagnosed with HIV, a disease that is new to our country and that eventually moves on to become AIDS. Sometimes people live for years with HIV. Unfortunately, when Dr Reid ran a test for antibodies, he found your dad has a fast-moving form of AIDS. If he lives out the year it will be surprising."

"But surely Dr Reid prescribed medicine for him?"

"He can only prescribe for the symptoms of the viruses. He can neither control nor stop their progression. There is no cure." Janet sobbed quietly as Gramps continued, "Physically he will waste away. He doesn't want us to see him in that state nor does he want our pity."

Dale's eyes glazed in shock; yet, he remembered his white water training when facing the unexpected: "Keep a firm grip on your paddle and continue a steady path." Still he wanted to run into the backyard screaming in frustration. He held his breath until the urge passed.

Luci, however, turned to Janet in astonishment, striking out in panic. "*You* caused this!" she screamed hysterically. "Can't you do something? I love Daddy. You drove him away. I hate you."

Janet reached out to hold her and wrestled with her, but Luci leapt away. Gramps, used to emergencies on the farm, quickly slapped Luci's face to snap her out of her hysteria.

"Apologize to your mother at once. You will respect your mother. She did *not* bring this on her household."

Luci placed her hand on the red mark on her cheek, weeping softly. Gramps lifted her like a baby and held her on the sofa until she cried through a box of Kleenex and his shirt was sopping wet. He held out his other arm for Janet to cry with them.

"We're going to make it with God's help," Gramps said.

"We'll learn about AIDS so we'll be prepared and not broadsided again. Your dad warned that there's a vast amount of fear and prejudice about AIDS because it's new and because people don't understand the way it spreads. They only know that it's deadly. People isolate not only those sick with it but also their companions and family. Therefore we are not to tell anyone—not even Mandy and Paul.

"The main fear is caused by not knowing how it's transmitted. You can't get it through casual contact or toilet seats. Last year Doris Day was photographed hugging Rock Hudson before he died of it, to prove touching didn't spread the disease."

Luci lifted her head to sniffle, "Mom, I'm sorry. I felt guilty because I hadn't visited Dad for a while—now it's too late. Forgive me."

Janet rose and sat beside Luci, holding her hand. Dale, vainly trying to brush away the tears, joined them.

Toby, who was sitting on his haunches at Luci's feet, raised his head and howled like a wolf calling its pack together.

36

End of April 1986

Bending forward with a slight permanent stoop, Ryan tried to buckle the belt on his once tight trousers. He couldn't find a notch tight enough to keep the pants up. 'Others are this thin,' he thought, 'they're called wiry. And they keep doing what needs to be done. It's my tiredness and dizziness. I can't seem to energize myself.'

He reached up to touch the one ornament suspended by wires from the ceiling—his canoe. "We rode those rapids well. Not once did you let me capsize."

By the sofa stood his paddle, his requisite partner in the water. Sitting on his gold easy chair, he grasped the wide-bladed paddle with his hand on the small top and swung it as though he glided into still waters. For a moment, his eyes shifted from memories of dark dens to raptured vistas of rivers running between verdant cliffs. When the paddle dropped from his slack hand, he woke with a start. Soon his frequent feeling of late surfaced. "I've gone under once and come back up. It's like drowning—three times and you're gone."

*   *   *   *   *

Tony downshifted into the church parking lot beaming at the pastor's empty reserve spot; then he braked at the side door beside Rita's Sunbird. As he entered the outer office she smiled at him, triggering a response of a slow motion jig and his best grin. While she talked on the phone he watched expressions chase across her face, then return to its customary calm. Because her joyous calmness attracted him the most, he knew it would

158

break his heart to see her cry. He couldn't continue to drop in without good excuses. Would he be missed if he didn't stop by?

Replacing the receiver, Rita turned to him. "How is your day going?"

"Well now that I see you, it's going better. I'd hoped to ask pastor to visit a young man currently in prison for a few days. I don't think he's the culprit, so properly guided he could become a good citizen. Is it your coffee break? Anyway, I brought you a large cup." He placed the coffee container directly in her hand, savouring the physical touch.

Rita's eyes swept over him. He really was a hunk. Far too handsome for his own good. If she went with him she'd buy sweat shirts that said "Property of Rita" to keep the pack at bay. When she first met the 'golden boy', she suspected he was all outer wrappings. Now she liked and respected him. He proved his determination to 'walk the walk', appearing at church whenever the doors opened. And his bass voice greatly added to their choir which suffered from lack of males. Gratefully she sipped her coffee while he talked, noting that he slipped in questions to learn more about her, cagily saying, "Did you do that too?" after describing a youthful escapade. In Tony's presence she felt feminine again—as though that part she buried with her husband was resurrecting. For safety she started to discuss work.

"Pastor did say to give you this envelope. It's business you both are concerned in. He seemed to know you would arrive." She tilted her head in puzzlement. "Thanks. The coffee and company are appreciated."

Pocketing the envelope, Tony blew her a kiss and left. 'He does that to all the girls,' she thought. Still, he was pleasant. She shrugged as she buried her thoughts in the pile of work. Pastor would return soon; he rarely was in his office when golden boy breezed in.

Later, on his way home Tony stopped at McDonald's hoping to see Dale in his 'salt mine'. At the cash register, Dale's smile never reached his eyes, for he wore a furrow of worry in his forehead.

"Has Luci all those dogs trained and exercised?"

"Oh yes. The only one getting fatter is Toby, who reads her like a fire hydrant."

Dale looked tense. Tony wondered why. Had Anna switched to another guy? But he doubted it. Taking his change he asked, "Is everything alright at home?"

Dale didn't mean to talk but it spurted out before he could clamp his lips shut. "We're making out okay. It's Dad who worries us. The only person he talks to is Gramps."

Tony froze. Ryan adored his children. What was going on? "Maybe I should call your mother tonight."

"Yes, please do. We need help. Here's your takeout. I put in extra french fries."

"Thanks. Give my love to Anna," Tony teased.

"No way. She only wants *my* love," Dale fired back.

"Good." Tony was pleased that in that quarter all was well.

After a quick drive home, Tony phoned Janet to discover why Ryan was not in touch with his children. Her straightforward answer: that Ryan had removed himself from their lives because he had contracted AIDS only partially surprised him. To diminish the underlying current of worry that he detected in her voice, he reassured her he would apply his superlative detecting skills and would locate Ryan.

Mid-May 1986

On the outskirts of town, unbeknown to Tony another concern steadily worsened. Ryan's hand shook, spilling drops of milk that for half an hour he had half-heartedly striven to drink. If he didn't look at it, his stomach seemed more accepting. Bites of bread and cheese lodged in his gullet, for which he was thankful. If they proceeded too quickly he developed diarrhoea.

He recalled his impeccable care of clothes and body. As a teenager he wore clothes one time then threw them in the wash. When he married Janet, he cared for his own clothes; always having pressed his trousers with a razor-sharp pleat. In his

160

carefully brushed jackets and spotless shirts he faced the world immaculately clothed. No longer.

Fatigue arrogantly ruled his body. Even his eyelashes hurt. Lacking energy reserves, the nine yard dash to the bathroom became impossible. At times, mounds of previous upheavals formed an obstacle course. He didn't understand why anything came out of his body, for he had no appetite. His skin hung as loosely on his arms as his unwashed clothes swung on his frame.

On bad days his mind recalled nothing more than a blur, waves of heat rising and warping the view. A crawl into bed helped to ease the tension, and he slept until 3 a.m. His haphazardly drawn drapes allowed motel lights to shine in. And weird shadows lurked in the corners. Ryan's pyjamas and sheets were soaked from night sweats. His throat burned like Death Valley; his body on fire from the fever. The bloody phlegm he coughed up until his ribs pained, resulted from his body's inability to fight symptoms of bacterial pneumonia.

Taking his phone he dialled 911. The medics understood saying, "Unlock your door. We'll rush you to the hospital." Exhausted but relieved, Ryan crawled to the door, unlocked it, then shivered on the floor. Within minutes the ambulance arrived and routed him to the hospital.

After Ryan was admitted and strung with intravenous and other tubes, the ambulance crew returned to their posts. "We got him just in time," they commented. Sipping coffee while they awaited their next emergency call, the driver jumped up reaching for the phone, "I promised this guy I'd tell him about our last call."

The number he dialled was for a downtown office. Although the recipient slept at home, the driver left a message on the answering service concerning the address of a Ryan Telfer.

The other medics shrugged with raised eyebrows, "God willing, let's hope he'll be going back to that address."

161

37

End of third week of May, 1986

In the house near Grand Park a light breeze blew the scent of lilacs through open bedroom windows, inducing pleased smiles on prone sleeping figures. Except in the master bedroom where the lone occupant tensed as she began to thrash from side to side.

Flinging her arms in front of her, Janet suddenly screamed: "STOP! STOP!" With her chest heaving as though she had run the one minute mile, her words awakened her from the nightmare. Gulping deep breaths of air, her shaking fingers turned on the bedside light.

Across the hall, Dale called sleepily, "Are you alright, Mom?"

"Yes, thank you dear. Only a dream. Go back to sleep."

But sleep eluded Janet, for she uncannily had re-dreamed a nightmare experienced two years previously. In it she tried to walk into the park but people fleeing past her yelled, "Don't go into Grand Park! They're throwing people into a bonfire!" She saw people moving steadily to a huge fire. Before she turned to run out of the park, she called out: "Stop!" to warn a group of figures moving like zombies towards the flames. Only one tall wraith of a man heard and looked back over his shoulder. Although he seemed familiar, she woke up before she could call him by name and bring him to safety.

She walked to the window and stared into the black depths of the opposite park. A few sleepy ducks riding in the calm water quacked among themselves. Willows gracefully bending over the

162

stream barely moved in the predawn breeze. What a serene landscape. This rerun of her nightmare left her calm and confident. To her surprise she was not afraid. Perhaps the man who heard her was Ryan. Maybe not. She'd better not get carried away—it would be too disappointing.

Snuggling in her bed she sleepily remembered she had applied for a position as vice principal if such a job opening came. It would be super to be a V.P. Teaching had become her life, for she poured vast amounts of energy into helping students achieve. As well, they'd have money for Dale's university fees. However, if she wasn't given the position, she'd be content in her classroom.

With a weary sigh she closed her eyes drifting back into sleep.

*　*　*　*　*

Tony's office was exactly as it always was at 8 a.m., no phone ringing, every filing cabinet's top cleared ready for the next case. With his latest investigation successfully wrapped up, Tony paused before emptying his overflowing in-basket. Spurning piles of papers that were so overdue for his attention and signature they could wait another few hours, he churned with thoughts of yielding to his bad case of spring fever. Nest-building birds flew in and out of their trees. Mare's tail clouds promised fair weather. Woods revived by fresh running sap seemed to be calling him. How long ago was it that he delighted in trilliums and picked mayflowers?

Oh well, this restlessness would have to wait. Hesitantly sipping his hot coffee he switched on his voice mail. "Sgt. Tony, last night we picked up a badly dehydrated Ryan Telfer, feverish with pneumonia and admitted him to General Hospital. The address we picked him up at was the Oakridge Motel, Riverside Road, Suite 2. We've kept our promise. Over."

Immediately alert, Tony whispered, "Thank you guys." The hospital line gave the busy signal, but Ryan would surely be there

163

for a week, maybe more. He'd wait until Ryan returned home before visiting him. No wonder he couldn't find him. He had unsuccessfully searched for his friend in apartment buildings. Because his own new self-identity in Christ brought him everything he longed for—the peace that transcends understanding and freedom in Jesus—he prayed for the man whom he devastated by his departure.

'Oh Ryan, I'm nothing. I hurt you. But you don't need me—you need Jesus, who can meet your needs and take away false guilt. Ryan, open your eyes and heart to Jesus' love.'

In his spirit, Tony heard Jesus say, "I've paid the price for you and for Ryan. Can you be part of my sufferings? Can you fight for Ryan's redemption?"

"I'm in fights all the time. What are You talking about?"

"Read Ephesians 6—not just with your intellect but until you grasp or understand it in your heart. You're in a fight for eternity for Ryan."

"That prophecy in last Sunday's service that stated: When we climb to the top of the mountain You will ask, 'Where is your brother?' that was for me, wasn't it?"

He knew Jesus smiled and his own heart leapt with joy—the same joy that took Jesus through the Cross.

The fourth week of May Tony drove to Ryan's address. From the highway the two-storied Oakridge Motel stretched non-descriptly, leaving only a driveway at each end of the lot. Tony hoped the rooms were decorated more elegantly than the drab outer shell. Surmising the suites were grouped at the far end near the office, he shifted his heavy brown bag so it wouldn't spill; walked to the door for #2, and knocked. After 5 minutes he rapped urgently again. No answer. Realising Ryan's virulent form of AIDS could keep him in bed, he knocked louder and louder until his knuckles turned red.

Finally, shuffling feet approached the door's other side. When it opened, Tony faced a spectre who was only half the size of the Ryan he knew. At least, he assumed the emaciated figure was Ryan.

"Oh it's you!" Ryan weakly said as though Tony were a low bellied reptile. Turning on his heels Ryan walked from the door to lie on his bed. Because he lacked strength to climb stairs, the bed now occupied the main floor.

Tony moved directly to the kitchen to recover from shock brought on by Ryan's appearance. His teeth were more prominent, as though they had slid forward a fraction; his eyes were hollow from retreating into his skull and he looked to weigh ninety pounds or less. He was just letting himself fade away; therefore, he had to get some nourishment into him.

From the groceries he carried, he took out a plastic container, and spooned out choice pieces of stew into a dish that he placed in the microwave. The remainder he divided into dishes to be heated by Ryan the next day.

On a large plate he placed the meal by Ryan's bedside. Fluffing pillows for him to lean against he said, "This is delicious lamb stew. Your favourite. Have you eaten today?"

"No. I haven't done much cooking."

Tony watched while his friend ate the meal one slow spoonful at a time. "Is anyone looking after you?"

"No." Ryan wanted to take refuge in the oblivion of his drugs for the rest of his life. He had no desire to cope with necessities.

"When you've finished eating would it be alright for me to wash your sores and change your sheets?"

"Okay. I could use help."

A fit of coughing that left him dizzy and faint forced Ryan to stop eating. Tony gently lowered Ryan's head on the bed, then righted him again to finish eating. Because it was a favourite meal he began to savour its nourishing taste. Meanwhile Tony searched for the suite's keys. He found one in Ryan's coat pocket.

"Tomorrow I'll return this key after I've had a duplicate made. You haven't any cleaning disinfectant. I'll bring some."

While Ryan was in the bathroom Tony stripped the bed, then

took the sheets to the laundry room to wash. Borrowing a broom he found there, he swept the top level of dirt from Ryan's downstairs floors. After he returned the broom he remade the bed with clean and sweet-smelling sheets. He wondered if the television should be moved nearer the bed, but he didn't ask.

Ryan plugged in the kettle for a cup of tea. As it brewed they faced each other in silence. Finally Ryan whispered, "You mean it, don't you. You're coming to look after me."

"Yes. When did you last eat a proper meal?"

"I think in the hospital, so they would allow me to come home."

They drained their cups silently in the manner of a Japanese tea ceremony thinking long thoughts about each other—only the deadly disease darkened their reflections.

38

Tony wanted only one thing—a secluded, dark hole to creep into where he could be alone and endure his remorse and pain in peace. Shock and helplessness because of the onslaught of AIDS in Ryan's body had replaced his initial elation at finding Ryan's hideaway. His listless, "I don't care any more" words hurt worse than any insults. He couldn't call him any name more lethal than ones Tony thought up for himself.

The culminating blow was the hell of despair and loneliness that stared at him from Ryan's eyes. When he isolated himself from the support of family and friends, he created a vacuum into which painful longings and morbid depression crawled. He seemed to no longer care about himself or his death sentence. Except as the two men drank their tea in relaxed peace, Ryan received a small degree of comfort such as is found in resting a broken arm.

After they emptied the teapot, Tony supported Ryan to his cot and checked that the phone, bedpan and other necessary items were within the patient's reach. Leaving him to undress and settle down, Tony assured him he would return the following evening. Then he stepped out the door breathing deeply fresh, oxygen-laden night air.

Above him stars still twinkled, a nearby dog barked, horns honked. Inside him a maelstrom of unanswered questions made his head spin. Who did he think he was to nurse such a sick man? But if he didn't take care of Ryan, who could or would? He was his brother—he must help him. Nothing in his former life had prepared him to become an all-in-one housekeeper and medic. Ryan's face haunted Tony. He longed to make him comfortable and to lessen his torment. To do that he needed expert advice.

Next morning, he veered his car into a driveway, turned it around and headed for the church. Nowadays his answers were found in that direction. As usual, Pastor Bob wasn't in his office. Tony smiled to himself, 'he must know when I'm coming.' However, Rita appeared from the inner office to greet him with a bright "Good morning." He briefly wondered if he should practise his recently discovered talent of carrying a tune by singing "Hello." But he didn't feel like singing and besides, he confined his rehearsing to his bathroom. Instead he curtly replied, "Good morning."

"You appear to think it isn't a good day."

Sitting on a corner of her desk, he agreed. "I've seen better. I've a lot on my mind."

"It's obviously heavy stuff. I'm a good listener." She shoved aside piles of papers, then looked expectantly at him. She gestured to a nearby chair.

Used to her guarded, brief responses, he studied her face and posture. What had he done to deserve her attention? Elsewhere another phone rang until the answering service clicked in. Rita waited, as poised as a sheep dog watching for orders from its shepherd.

Tony wondered, did she realise what his problem was? Maybe she was a mind reader. Then he recalled that she had nursed her husband when he was fatally ill with cancer. Having been a care giver, she knew the ins and outs of tending a patient.

He longed to blurt out his distress and inadequacy to handle looking after Ryan. Still he hesitated. How much did she know about the former Tony? Would she be shocked?

When he raised his head to refute any need of help, he glimpsed tears in her eyes. His own watered suspiciously.

"I know when someone is hurting. That's the time you need friends. How can I help?"

168

Tony breathed deeply. "Do you know about my past?"

"What past? That's under Jesus' blood. Are you helping your former boyfriend?"

Tony stood and walked to the window, staring out with unseeing eyes. What a tangle! If he told her about Ryan's debilitating AIDS and how he visited him, would she react with the blinding fear held by most people? He was falling in love with this woman. If she rejected him, he'd be crushed.

At her desk Rita watched sadly and patiently until several minutes limped by. "Tony, come and sit down. Because I type Pastor Bob's minutes, I'm sworn to secrecy on the Bible. That applies to this conversation, too. Please trust me."

With great relief, he turned around the chair opposite the desk in order to sit on it astride. "Rita, you're an angel. Of course, I trust you but I was loath to upset you. Your female intuition operates in perfect working order. I desperately need advice on the best way to care for an extremely ill man."

He paused, then added softly, "My ex-boyfriend is dying of AIDS."

For two quick breaths Rita's expression softened, and she was half rising as if to place her arms around him. Then she resumed her secretarial stance and took aim at the issue.

"My husband died an unpleasant, painful death—devoured by cancer. However they die you share their suffering. Because I nursed Joe, I understand the difficulties—the stress. And I'm honoured that you trust me."

'Tony gaped open-mouthed.

"Yes. We'll make a list of necessary items. Is he bedridden?"

"Most of the time. Lack of appetite and diarrhoea have left him weak and thin. Sometimes he uses the bathroom or bedpan. Often he doesn't move quickly enough."

"Have you ever nursed someone before?"

"No. And he refuses to have his family see him in this terrible condition. Also, he fears the pariah-like treatment of AIDS victims would victimize their lives. I tracked him down in his isolation. Not his idea! Because he needs care, he submits to my evening visits."

"Poor man. Tony, you're the angel—not me." She waved her tooth-marked pencil. "Let's see. You need to rent a hospital bed. I'll phone around to find one at a reasonable price.

"Bedding—with such frequent changes, you'll need a mountain of sheets available. I'll tap some ladies for their old sheets so you'll need to wash them only once a week. That leaves your dinners. When he eats so little, they must be twice as nourishing. Also, good food will keep *you* healthy. Do you agree?"

"Yes."

She had just shredded all his perplexing problems as if they were merely piles of grass. Feeling out of his depth he rested his chin on the chair back and watched her.

Disregarding him, Rita planned strategies like a crusading suffragette. Still wielding her sharp pencil, she listed church women who would provide meals.

"Fortunately, our church kitchen has a freezer that will hold a week's supply of dinners for you two. The women will happily cook an extra portion and a half ready for pick-up after Sunday service. Since I'm a soup expert, there'll always be a variety of tasty soups or stew in the freezer. They will tempt your friend's taste buds."

Tony saw a light at the end of his dark tunnel. "How can I ever thank you?"

"Don't try. We do it for Jesus. However, tell us your patient's preferences to forestall lack of interest in food and loss of appetite. And you pace yourself. Don't become overtired. Also buy up a supply of rubber gloves."

"I'll do that."

Outside a car stopped near the side door; ladies' voices hummed in the sanctuary. The ongoing life of the organism called a church throbbed into their personal space, ending their encounter.

After Tony rose and left whistling "Amazing Grace", Rita slumped at her desk.

170

At last tears were allowed to race down her cheeks.

*   *   *   *   *

Tony drove on back streets to his office, stalling for time to reset his mind to police duties. Bradley would have set strategies in place for their new assignment, Tony's only information being that it was an ecstasy lab in an old warehouse. But at headquarters, on entering Bradley's office, he picked up a hefty file and was greeted by a partner beaming at his arrival.

"Glad you're here. I've sent Jim to learn who owns this warehouse, but he hasn't got back yet. How are you managing with Ryan? Is he in the hospital?"

"No, but it's okay—my personal business is organized so that if necessary I'll squeeze feeding Ryan and changing his bedding into an hour during the evening. Otherwise, I'm with you on this ecstasy lab assignment. That stuff is sold at rave dances. Are you a good dancer?"

"Very funny. We have the ID of the drug pusher. A lab company who sold secondhand equipment to this guy asked him where he had his lab. He gave a bullshit answer and refused to have them carry his purchase to his car so they couldn't read his licence number. However, he came back again in a couple of weeks so they were able to alert us and we followed him."

"That gives us good surveillance opportunities. I presume there are wiretaps in this warehouse. What about his car?"

"Yes, we have placed taps generously in the warehouse, in his apartment and in neighbouring phone booths, but not in his rental car."

"Great. Then you and I, right now, should visit the rental company to get their cooperation to put a tap in an upgrade of his car. Then they will call him in and give him the upgrade."

"I'm with you—let's go. In your folder is a surveillance plan for you to check. If there's any inconvenience we can adjust the times and locations.

"Okay. This is top priority. I'm really grateful to you, Brad,

171

for your master planning. We'll talk in greater detail while we stake him out."

Bradley gave him an understanding jab with his knuckles and a chin-up grin. "We're relentless. We always get the job done."

* * * * *

On Sunday morning, bracing himself lest Rita's plans failed to culminate, Tony steered around chatting parishioners to visit the freezer at the rear of the kitchen. Lifting its lid he spotted a sizable box marked 'Tony Express' in which were packed carefully marked containers labelled: soup, stew, lasagna and similar home cooking. With a whoop he picked it up, knowing Ryan would be pleased, since he himself lacked time to cook meals.

Further inspection revealed an apple pie placed on top as if to fill the space. How did she know apple pie was his favourite? More pleased than he cared to admit, he set a course for the parking lot. But a tap on the shoulder interrupted his exit.

"Not speaking to me any more, Tony Moretti?" Anna stood with hands on hips. "Dale misses your drop-in visits at McDonald's." She waited for an explanation with her eyes glued to the carefully held box.

"I assumed you were in Dale's good hands," Tony winked at her.

"What are you up to carrying that box of food?"

"I had a yen for home cooked meals. How did you know this box contained food?" Tony eyed her suspiciously.

"My mother cooked a few of the meals … so I hope you talk to Dale about his father. We're not babies—we've read about that disease and know what is fact and what is hysteria concerning the way it's spread."

Tony groaned. He might be a good detective but as a secret

service agent he'd be a cop-out. "Anna, perhaps I'll be allowed to answer Dale's questions. I don't know. Tell him to be patient." With a pat on the frustrated girl's shoulder, he strode out the door to his car. Over his shoulder he called, "Thank your mother for me."

Anna shook her fist.

39

Gramps leaned back on the stone bench silently watching quivering leaves on maple trees that guarded Wifey's grave. For a few moments he yearned for her soft touch and reassuring laughter. Since her death ten years ago, distressing events had become the norm, especially in their son's life. They caused Gramps on one hand to wish for her comforting wisdom, but on the other hand he was relieved she didn't have to go through the trauma of Ryan's divorce and his fatal illness. If the doctor's prediction proved correct, this summer Ryan's grave would be dug beside hers in this hillside cemetery.

Kneeling by her gravestone he yanked a few weeds from the rosebush garden he had planted. With pride he noted the many buds forming on the bush. Maybe next Sunday en route to his weekly dinner with Janet and the children, he'd pick a few roses to take to his ladies. In their pleasure they'd hug him until like Toby he shook himself free to regain his composure.

"Well love," he told Sarah, "I'd best be going to town. Janet's a wonderful cook. Like you she not only cooks the Sunday dinner, she also provides a Care package for most of my meals during the week. Since Ryan isolated himself and only phones me, they count on me to bring news of him to these laid-on dinners. Unfortunately, I'm in the dark, too, for he rarely tells me the disease's full progress. I only guess that the disease is winning—he is going downhill rapidly. What a tamasha!"

Resisting tears, Gramps wove between graves to his rusty but faithful truck. 'Guard her well,' he nodded to the sheltering trees. The Ford engine roared into life venting its usual gurgles before settling into a speedy rhythm. 'The family never accuses me of sneaking up on them.' He chuckled. But a confusion of thoughts teemed through his mind as he recalled the past week's phone conversation with Ryan. Should he repeat it verbatim, giving them the newest circumstance, or should he stick to his usual "he's as well as can be expected" speech?

Botheration! He extracted his ever-present pipe from his outer pocket, stuck it in his mouth and sucked on it like an Indian peace pipe. Concentrating on traffic he wondered whether the family would condemn or support Ryan.

Three o'clock almost to the second, Janet heard Gramps' truck pound into the driveway, noisy as a Piper airplane, then clank to a stop. Leaping to her feet to check her pork roast and accompanying vegetables in the oven, she listened for Luci's pit-a-pat on the stairs.

When she swept into the kitchen she proudly announced, "I remembered, Momma, and I'm right on time to make the tea. I hope Gramps has real news for us, unlike the way he fudges over Dad's illness."

Janet gave her a quelling look that was unheeded by Luci, who was engrossed in her tea-making duties, carefully selecting Gramps' favourite cake and cookies. She glared at Dale and slapped his hand that was poised over a date square. "You'll have one when the tea is poured."

Dale shrugged and opened the door for Gramps as he entered the kitchen. Suddenly the older man's creased brow, his stooped shoulders, his frailness, alarmed him. "Gramps, it's so good to see you. Let's sit on the sofa."

With Toby in position between them they looked hopefully at Luci. She placed the sweets tray near their grandfather, then poured the freshly made tea into their cups. To reach her tea Janet pulled a chair closer. Savouring its warmth she exchanged the usual courtesies regarding health, weather and crops. As soon as the teenagers, to Gramps' amusement, had claimed most of the cookies, their bodies tensed apprehensively, waiting for their guest to report on their father.

Gramps drank the rest of his tea.

"What I have to say, you've heard before. Ryan phones at least once a week so I know he's still alive. If he's having a good day, he's alert and his voice is normal. If he has a fever or is heavily sedated for pain, I don't recognize his voice. His world has narrowed to this disease. Mainly he asks for news about you. I tell him about our Sunday dinners and your escapades. Sometimes he talks about the past. I think he has deep regrets which add to his suffering."

"What is Dr Reid's diagnosis on his present condition? If we phoned him would he answer our questions? Not knowing is torturing us." Janet sat forward without moving her eyes from Gramps' face. A light breeze wafted the curtains in and out at the open window while the motionless family ignored their tea.

"I can't answer for Dr Reid—I doubt he'd betray Ryan's wishes. I think he would like to give us his diagnosis, so we could care for him; but it's Ryan's call."

Dale pushed Toby off the sofa in order to face Gramps. "Has anyone seen Tony recently? He used to pop into McDonald's on his way home from work. But recently he hasn't come in. I've asked other workers to watch for him and let me know. He seems to have disappeared, too."

A twitch appeared in Gramps' left cheek.

Dale declared: "Anna suspects he is seeing Dad. Her mother is one of the church ladies asked to prepare a portion and a half meals—must be nutritious—for a sick male. On Sunday she followed Tony who went to the church freezer and took out a box of food containers. What's more, he refused to answer her questions. Gramps, if Tony found Dad and is seeing him, Dad must have told you. Come on—we have a right to know."

Gramps frowned for a moment, then his face cleared as he understood he had to tell them. He had no recourse except to repeat Ryan's story. He admired Anna's sleuthing. But noting everyone's suspended breathing he opted to quickly ease their

176

tension.

"Yes. Ryan says Tony showed up at his door, walked in and announced he was going to look after him. Every evening he feeds your father, washes him and his bedding, and tries to alleviate his pain. Thanks to the ladies of Tony's church he has home-cooked nutritious meals for himself and for Ryan."

Glancing at Dale he added, "You may tell Anna the meals are much appreciated, although Ryan's appetite is meagre."

While the news was not heartening, they were relieved that Dad was being looked after. As they absorbed the news, Janet silently sought Gramps' hand and he squeezed hers. Luci leaned against Dale's knee, grateful that he had wrung the information from Gramps. Unspoken thoughts that flitted to the fore were banished lest tears destroy the calm. Whatever befell their family in the future, for now they drew comfort from mutual love and shared suffering.

Toby participated by sniffing a tantalizing aroma coming from the oven. Janet laughed, "Time to renew our physical strength. Wash your hands for the feast."

Between bites of pork and squash, Gramps said, "Tony brings news about you to Ryan; although when he isn't in direct touch with you he may be vague on some details. The problem is he spends most of his off hours with Ryan, making him unavailable to the family."

"I'm going to leave a message on Tony's answering service requesting ways in which we can help. If we can't help Ryan maybe we can contribute by helping Tony. At the very least they will feel our support."

Luci nodded, "I feel so miserable. Maybe I can volunteer at the General Hospital running errands. Do you think that would please Dad?" She glanced around to catch their subtle reactions.

Gramps brightened, giving her a warm smile. Dale fixedly studied a smudge on the ceiling and Janet hugged her proudly.

"Let's concentrate on your father; later you can tour the hospital to see if you'd like to do that. For now, we'll work together sending messages with Gramps and finding ways of helping."

Outside a semi-trailer squealed its brakes; a boom box blared a Michael Jackson song until its owner rounded a corner.

At last, Gramps exchanged glances with Janet, and with the defiance of an old rooster proclaimed, "Ryan needs us. Why should we be imprisoned by other people's prejudices? Our love for Ryan is greater than fear of AIDS."

40

Tony returned to the motel on Concession Street. Lest a family friend follow him, he drove a longer route. Discovery of Ryan's address could traumatize him and end their fragile relationship. Thus, each time Tony came and went, he scanned the cars parked by rented units. Always licence plates for neighbouring states and Canada hung on the autos which travelling sales reps drove.

The suite at the motel's far end looked peaceful, even golden in the rays of the setting sun. In June the long daylight brought walkers with their leashed dogs trotting on extended tours that included Concession Street. A few overnighters lolled under a nearby maple tree and ate their Kentucky Fried Chicken. The night personnel opened the office screen door to the cries of "What kept you? I'm glad you're here. My daughter is in a recital tonight." And the day staff woman raced to her car.

Inside the motel suite, the curtains were closed for greater privacy. At the dinette table uneaten food among a jungle of boxes and papers looked like a small-scale garbage dump. When Ryan greeted him from the easy chair by the bed, Tony discerned his thin shape in the twilight zone.

.   Ignoring Tony's surprised "Hey! Hey! You're up and living," Ryan spoke in flat, listless tones: "Don't be deceived. With great effort I've made tea—there's some in the teapot."

While Tony stowed the frozen dinners in the freezer compartment, Ryan sipped tea—much needed liquid—into his mouth. "Tired ... I'm so tired," he mused, "even when morphine

179

kills the pain so I sleep, I wake up hung over. It's painful to breathe, to sit up, to move my arms . . ."

He fretted about his morphine dosage which he hoped Dr Reid would increase on Tuesday. Lost in his foggy thoughts he heard Tony mention 'a hospital bed.' Good grief! Why does he rant about a hospital bed? His senses alerted by his steely determination to avoid such a move, he listened to Tony's announcements.

"The ladies at the church collected a pile of sheets, so no matter the number of emergencies you have, clean bedding will be on your bed. I know you're able to sit in a chair while I change your bed, but you're more than ready now to lie down again. Perhaps I should learn to change the sheets with you in them as they do in hospitals. Maybe I could do it without increasing your pain."

From under his eyelids Ryan heard the microwave whirring to heat their supper; the snap of rubber as fingers wriggled into work gloves, the gurgle of disinfectant being poured down the sink.

Once the depressing sickness smell was replaced by sanitary clean odours that refreshed the air like a spring breeze, Tony's breathing pattern changed from shallow breaths to gulps of oxygen. His appetite also returned, reminding him to extract the dinners from the microwave and place one on a tray for Ryan in his chair and his own on the table. He refilled the two-thirds empty large water pitcher beside Ryan's bed.

Within minutes Tony devoured his meat loaf and veggies. Whereas Ryan strove to swallow a few spoonfuls of the thick carrot soup, and winced at attempts to raise his hand. Tony knelt beside him to steady his arm and helped him drain the bowl. In Ryan's mouth, his tongue coated white from thrush bacteria made swallowing an effort.

"If I eat a lot, my stomach churns and my bowels flow. Even this home cooking tastes like sawdust. I am trying." But he put down his spoon and shut his eyes, exhausted.

"I'm starting to write down what you eat. The ladies want to learn your preferences to create delicious meals for you. They'll feel miserable because you ate only three mouthfuls. Even if the food just passes straight through you, some nutrition must stay in your body." With sudden inspiration he added, "Tomorrow I'll bring pablum which I'll mix up so you can work away at it during the day. Your water intake is fine."

"Dr Reid emphasized 'drink water until it comes out your ears'. I find it easy to drink some every time I wake up from a snooze.

"Did you know Anna saw you at the church with the box of dinners? When I phoned Dad to listen to his recount of the Sunday dinner, he told me you were the hot topic. Dale thinks you know my address and are visiting me."

"Anna waylaid me as I was taking out the dinners. I didn't tell her anything. I didn't know they put the pieces together. I presume they want into the action. They're very determined and wily. They love you—you're their Dad. How would you feel if Gramps were sick somewhere and you neither knew where nor were asked to help him? You'd be all over the place to find him."

Ryan's chin sank to his chest. He'd never thought about how the family felt. In his precautions for their safety, he'd realised only the physical and social dangers. What should he do? He knew he called out for them in his sleep—he loved and missed them every moment.

"Ryan, with the best of intentions, you have shut them out of your life. They miss you—you're their beloved father. They need to share the bad experiences as well as the good times you've had. Especially since this AIDS epidemic is new, they imagine far worse things than the truth is. They are both growing up—no longer carefree teenagers. Luci even plans to register as a volunteer at the General Hospital.

"As for you, you're so stoic and undemanding; you're a good patient—a good model."

Male voices discussing where to eat dinner passed the door. Further away a car door slammed. Ryan shook his head slightly and tried to stand.

"What can they do for me that you aren't doing?"

"They can talk with you on the phone; they can spend precious time with you that they never can again—valuable time because of its limitations. They can comfort you and share your suffering. That's a wonderful gift of love on both sides.

"They realise you're fatally sick and they accept it. What they refuse to accept is being excluded by one of the most important persons in their young lives. To them it is not acceptable. They want to be treated as adults. Furthermore, you can't stop them. Unless I rent a car Dale could follow me here. I haven't time to drive in and out to shake another car off my trail."

Tony adeptly stripped the bed within seconds, then stuffed the bedding in a closet to be washed on the weekend. Clean sheets and a bed pad quickly replaced them. With his arm around Ryan he helped him weave the short distance to the bed. When he lay on his stomach to be bathed, Tony noted more purplish Kaposi's sarcoma spots had appeared. So gently he scarcely touched the feverish skin he washed and rinsed, particularly his genitals. Then he covered them with a diaper.

Other activities could wait, for Tony was ready to drink his tea while Ryan half sat and half lay on his bed. Pillows arranged with Tony's newfound technique that caused less pain surrounded Ryan's ninety pound body. Tony talked about his new case, about Rita's contribution and asked about the family.

In need of one of his short snoozes, Ryan regurgitated the information Gramps had given him. Tony replied, "That news isn't much to go on. You were always perceptive about your kids. You better phone them tomorrow."

"I'll sleep on it. Good night."

The next day while Ryan thought about contacting his family, a lovely floral arrangement was delivered to Tony's desk with a request it be taken to Ryan. As well as taking the bouquet with him that evening, he packed an overnight bag, an air mattress and sleeping bag, his most useful equipment from white water canoeing days. Unsure of Ryan's reaction he wondered whether the sick man would feel Tony had overstepped his welcome.

182

Regardless of his reception, he had to follow Dr Reid's orders, and he whistled to encourage himself.

Ryan stared at the unexpected bouquet that filled his doorway. Opening the card, he scanned it and tears began rolling down his face. Then he read it aloud to Tony: "Dad, these posies are a small indication of the fullness of our love for a wonderful father."

"Place them on the lower steps of the staircase beside my bed where I can breathe in their scent and appreciate their beauty."

Only after they ate their dinner, with Ryan eating more bites than usual, did he notice the bedroll and travel bag in a corner by the door. "What is that?"

"Well I talked to Dr Reid today. We discussed your medication as well as other needs. He said that someone should be with you during the night hours; so, I've come prepared to sleep overnight. The middle of the night or early morning is a low period. Fortunately, I'm a light sleeper—any sounds of distress will wake me up, so I can dial 911."

Tony braced for Ryan's extensive repertoire of abusive words. None came.

Between the flowers and the overnight nursing, Ryan looked as if he had won the lottery.

"Tony, you'll never know how alone and frightened I've felt during long dismal nights. I'm unable to control my body, causing so much stress that sometimes even breathing is difficult. Having you here, knowing I'm looked after, takes away the fear. Make yourself comfortable.

"I'm phoning Dale and Luci right now to say 'I love you'."

41

Janet, surprised the teenagers had not answered the phone, picked up the receiver on the sixth ring.

"Hello. Telfer residence." Silence at the other end nearly caused her to replace the phone; then a thin wavering voice said, "Hello Janet. May I speak to the kids?"

"Ryan! Oh praise God! Is it really you? I'll call them. We've needed to hear from you."

Ryan whispered, "Wait a minute. I want you to know I am so vastly sorry for my actions. At one time we did love each other."

"Yes, Ryan. Thank you. Thank you. I forgave you long ago. It was just too much for you to withstand your temptations. And in our youthful superiority, we made mistakes—we thought we had the answers. But we hadn't a clue about love and sex. Still, we had happy times. At least I did. Plus, you gave me two wonderful children. I hear Dale on the upstairs phone. Maybe we can talk again."

Luci was already grasping the receiver. "You liked the flowers! Cool!"

Janet escaped to her recently blooming roses. Because their velvety petals reminded her of God's truth and presence, she hoped some roses formed part of Ryan's bouquet. It was a relief to finally confront this illness instead of having it hanging over them like an unknown menace. They wanted to share Ryan's suffering. Being shut out so abruptly without any inkling or information punished them beyond reason. Thanks to Gramps they weren't at one another's throats.

Still, Luci's sobbing into her pillow at night and Dale's tense face had grabbed her heart. Ryan's hiding away with the instinct of an animal finding a hole in which to die alone, the callousness of it, had threatened to destroy their natural feelings of mortality and perhaps immortality.

Ryan's tragedy like a diuretic had cleansed their emotions so they knew how much they loved him. Love was never wasted. Because of it their faith remained strong.

"Mom," Luci yelled, "Daddy says we can visit him soon, but Tony warned it would have to be one of Dad's good days."

From the upstairs window, Dale shouted, "Let's have a pow-wow in the family room."

"Right on. In two minutes."

In the room, Luci bubbled on and on. "Daddy misses us. Loves the flowers. Hopes we visit him soon. Maybe it will help him get stronger."

Dale's body tightened. "It'll be great to see Dad, but we can't be shocked at his appearance. He's lost so much weight he's bound to look different. And if we look as though nothing is wrong, that's phony. So what do we do?"

"Was it hard to talk to him on the phone, even though his voice was so weak?" Janet asked.

"No, we picked up from when we last visited him."

"Luci, all your emotions—every one of them—shows on your face," Dale said. "We'll have to put a bag over your head—maybe a veil? Mom, let me visit first and take a photo so she'll be less surprised."

"At my drama classes I'll ask how to hide my shock. I don't want to hurt Dad. I'm so keen to see him."

"It would certainly be good if you could. Then seeing him ravaged by this sickness won't interfere with you talking, holding his hand. Loving him. Your dad knows he risks reactions but believes your love is so strong he won't care. He's realising time is precious. He wants to be with you while he can.

"There is a way to prepare so you can be normal and not embarrassed. Shut your eyes. Now picture your dad as you know him—tall, broad shouldered, lopsided grin, virile, maybe teasing you. Hold that picture. Bring it to the fore often. Then it will be so impressed on your mind that you won't be distressed."

Luci laughed.. "He's wearing that duck shirt that we pretended to dislike because it was so Walt Disney, and he's holding out his arms to me."

"He's prepared to canoe in white water and he's watching me so I'll learn. He's strong and resourceful. I always liked that in him."

"That's your dad. Hold that picture. I'll get out the albums so you can find other photos to refresh your memory. Dale, will you phone Gramps to take you both on the weekend. He knows his son and will whisk you out of there when Ryan is tired."

"Aren't you coming, too?"

"Not this time. Maybe I can help Tony nurse him when school's out. We'll see."

Toby ambled over to Janet to nuzzle her hand. Patting his head she felt he understood their sorrow. Her children faced the knowledge that they, too, were mortal—doomed to die. Soon they would be adults. Would they soar valiantly or would they settle for being safe?

*   *   *   *   *

The last week of June

With a thermometer in his mouth, Ryan waited for Tony to finish fluffing his many pillows into a supportive arrangement. He felt his senses dulled because of a morphine pill that also fogged his brain. In spite of dopiness, he smiled at the memory of his children's visit along with Gramps the previous Sunday. Gramps hugged him as if he were still his small son; he almost expected him to talk baby talk to him. And he in turn viewed his offspring as the little children they no longer were.

They had overflowed with love and delight at visiting him. Although Luci struggled valiantly not to show surprise and shock at his appearance, her wide eyes clouded over with pain. But she did not cry. Her voice squeaked as she relived tales of Toby's tricks until she grabbed his hand. He realised she wanted to make him laugh at her as he used to. So he ruffled her hair and grinned broadly. To laugh would have hurt his chest, which already had congestion.

To demonstrate their canoeing strokes Dale swung the paddle in ever-increasing arcs, barely missing Gramps, who ordered him to put that infernal device down. However, with each stroke Ryan and Dale remembered exciting, happy days on white water rivers. Their memories united them and he hoped that even after death a part of himself lived on in this tall, promising young man. Both his children would carry his love with them. How good it was to see them! Because they must have forgiven him, they would surely leave the unpleasantness behind.

A coughing fit which Ryan blamed on water going down the wrong way, alerted Gramps to leave him to rest. Before they opened the door, Ryan held the hand of each of his children and told them he loved them and was proud of them. They promised to return the next weekend.

Only four more days, for now it was Tuesday evening. Opening his eyes he heard Tony report, "I've phoned Dr Reid who is coming right away. You may need to go to the hospital. Your temperature is high."

Ryan groaned. He was too weak to argue with Tony; he'd save his strength to refuse the doctor.

Dr Reid, whose manner was brusque to conceal his feelings of helplessness, pinpointed the problem at once. "Tony told me you have both abdominal cramps and vomiting—guaranteed to deplete your body's resources. You have a 104 degree fever. If it increases, your body, which is already burning up, won't be able to handle it. I'm giving you a penicillin shot now and another one later in the hospital."

"No. I'm too weak. My body feels such pain with movement. No. Please let me stay here. Tony will stay with me and bathe me to bring the fever down."

Dr Reid peered over his smudged glasses at Tony, who nodded. "In the hospital your chance of survival is greater. The fever can be cured and intravenous will build you up. Tony, monitor him carefully. Hopefully the penicillin will save him at his fever's crisis point."

"Yes. I will monitor him carefully and try to bring down the fever."

"Okay for this once. He can have a reprieve, but in a few days we must take him to the Palliative Care unit. There it's brighter, peaceful and amenable for visiting relatives. Good night." Casting a doubtful look at Tony, he shook his head.

A grateful but confused Ryan touched Tony's hand, then slipped into a delirious sleep.

42

Outside, late comers to the motel parked by their rooms, slammed car doors, whistled tunelessly as they carried in luggage. Neither Ryan nor Tony heard their arrivals—Tony napped from exhaustion; Ryan dreamed in the morphine never land. Once the phone rang, but Tony dazedly knocked the receiver off to quell its shrillness. Spotlights at each of the motel's corners created pools of light surrounded by dense shadows. Like abandoned exiles, the men slept.

At midnight, Tony rearranged Ryan's blankets and took his temperature—over 104 degrees. Tony spooned water into Ryan's parched lips, tipping his head back to help the liquid slide down his throat. As well he stroked the moisture-soaked body with rubbing alcohol to lower the fever.

Seeing the hopelessness of his ministrations, he cried out to God, calling on Him to intervene, to restore Ryan's mind and body. "Not yet, God. He's not ready. Heal him, Lord."

At 1 a.m. Ryan shook with chills. After Tony placed a hot water bottle to draw blood to his feet, he wrapped his arms around Ryan, comforting him like a child. "Hang in there, buddy. You'll make it. You can beat this fever; Ryan, keep breathing." After a coughing attack, Ryan's breaths came in shallow gasps.

By 2 a.m. Ryan grew limp and lifeless—just lying in his bed —burning up. Tony commanded his patient, "Don't die, Ryan. Come back to us. Live, Ryan! You're not at peace with God. You can't die and leave that burden on your family. Oh God, let him live until his soul is at peace. Ryan stay here. Can you hear me? **Stay here!"**

At 3 o'clock as the breathing came with longer gaps in between, a desperate Tony cried out, "God, take me. I know You. I'm more prepared to die than Ryan. You've never allowed me to mention Jesus to him, so he doesn't know You. But I do. Heal him, Lord. You're the great Healer. Don't let him die."

With tears pouring down his face, Tony rose from kneeling to take Ryan's limp hand. It felt different.

When Tony mopped Ryan's brow, the skin no longer burned with heat. The fever had broken. At the crisis Ryan's body temperature dropped and his mind cleared. Opening his eyes he asked for water. Tony wrapped him warmly in dry pyjamas and a blanket, placing him on the sofa. Then he stripped the soaked sheets from the bed, giving thanks for the reprieve.

The rest of the night both men dozed. At half-hour intervals or whenever Ryan awoke Tony spooned broth as well as water into him to prevent dehydration. In the morning Dr Reid returned with more pills and the admonition that Tony had missed his calling, "You should have been a nurse."

A weak Ryan agreed. The doctor gave him a pill that would keep him asleep for the day, thus enabling Tony to go to his job without worrying about him.

That evening Tony brought clean sheets and a specially blended vegetable soup for Ryan.

When Tony finished his chores, Ryan asked, "When I was delirious, I thought I heard you talking. I even imagined you asked God to take you and save me? Did you?"

Tony glanced at him, his eyes bright and embarrassed, "Well, maybe I was delirious, too."

"I see—maybe you were." Ryan lay back and stared unseeingly at the ceiling, his hands clutching the sheet's edge anxiously.

Ryan awoke to a room partially glowing in sunlight that was wafted in through the open kitchen window. Birds guiding

190

fledglings rehearsed their songs over the steady hum of the antique refrigerator. Foreign accents spoken by people wandering towards the office came from beyond the front door.

All unrelated to him. He couldn't fathom why he lay in a bed in that motel. He was glad to be moving to the Palliative Care section in the General Hospital the next day. He centred the nosepiece of his oxygen tank appreciating normal breathing. Seeing his family restored a perspective to his problems. A poet said: "You can't be human alone." He adapted that to say, "You can't be sick alone."

Beside his bed he discovered a thermos of tea. Gratefully he poured himself a cup. He watched the steam rise and disappear into the air. "When I die will I, too, rise into the air and disappear? I almost found out last night. I know Tony prayed God would take him and not me because I'm not ready. Why? Dying doesn't take preparation—once you die, that's it. At least, there'll be no more pain. But I shall find out." His lips barely moved. as he whispered the words. "I don't want to go through this torture a second time."

After a few hours' sleep, blaring honks woke him and he settled into a new frame of mind. What an arrogant fool he was! When Tony rejected him, his wounded pride kept him angry and bitter, like a sore full of pus that grew sorer and bigger because he wouldn't let it drain. No more. He did so much for him, he forgave him. No longer was he angry; only ashamed that he had been so childish. Tony obviously made the right choice, for he was a different person from the man Ryan had slept with. He had it together—he had found himself. Ryan wanted that special strength Tony had.

At five o'clock Tony arrived to warm a nourishing, easy to swallow dinner. To his surprise he found Ryan sitting comfortably on the sofa and listening to but not watching television. As though he waited for him, he immediately clicked off the TV and motioned for Tony to sit beside him.

Looking him in the eye he said, "Tony, go ahead, tell me about Jesus."

191

Epilogue

After Ryan asked Jesus into his heart, his move to a bright homey room in the Palliative Care unit meant his family could drop in to see him at any time. He found that Jesus, who bore great pain on the cross, helped him endure his torment. As well, specialized nursing administered his morphine at regulated intervals without any in-between lapses.

Janet and Luci visited after four o'clock. On one occasion when they smuggled Toby in, he woofed away so excitedly to Ryan that they had to take him to the car. Dale looked in whenever he could, occasionally bringing Anna with him. She always gave Ryan a big hug that surprisingly never caused him to cry out in pain.

Gramps usually spent the entire day in his room—going to the cafeteria when others showed up. When he tried to share his faith he stumbled for words. But he knew he believed—Wifey had taught him, and he asked his son to tell her, when she welcomed him into Glory, that he held fast to his faith.

During Pastor Bob's visits, Ryan not only received counselling but also sound biblical teaching. The pastor taught him to talk to Jesus as a friend, always praying with him before he left.

Tony, who looked more rested, brought his lunch and Bible

every noon. They read the Word together and searched for more of Jesus, whose love Ryan now knew and whom he loved, too. As Ryan's morphine dosage increased and he was too drugged to talk, Tony still came to read the Word to him.

Two weeks from the day he received Jesus, Ryan's hiatuses in his breathing became longer as his organs were shutting down. The nurses phoned two persons. Tony arrived first. Sitting beside Ryan he watched his breathing become slower with longer intervals between each breath. Then another person entered the room. She gently touched Tony's shoulder before sitting in a chair with a book to read.

To answer Tony's quizzical look, Rita said, "Pastor Bob had the nurses phone me, too. I wanted to come, for I know the loss of a loved one."

After reading her book for ten minutes she raised her head, "The angels are here." She spoke in awe. "The early Christians said this is the time when the holy angels come to carry you to Glory."

A few minutes later she looked around, sensing the Presence, "Jesus is here."

Ryan's breaths stopped. Tony clasped Rita's hand—sharing the peace of Ryan's homecoming.